A. M. HOMES is the author of the novels *May We Be Forgiven, This Book Will Save Your Life, Music for Torching, The End of Alice, In a Country of Mothers* and *Jack*, a previous collection of short stories, *The Safety of Objects,* and the highly acclaimed memoir *The Mistress's Daughter*, as well as the travel memoir *Los Angeles: People, Places, and the Castle on the Hill*. She is a contributing editor to *Vanity Fair* and writes frequently on arts and culture for numerous magazines and newspapers. She lives in New York City.

'I loved A. M. Homes's stories in *Things You Should Know*' Adam Thirlwell, *Observer* Books of the Year

'Superlative examples of the form . . . these are stories you should read' *Sunday Times*

'There's weird and there's dark and then there are the stories of this highly original and terrifying writer . . . The magic comes with the smile of a killer and a slash of steel' *Irish Times* Fiction of the Year

'Proof of the contemporary robustness and elasticity of the form' Ali Smith, *Times Literary Suppplement*

'The writing is precise and witty – and the ideas are explored with intelligence and compassion' *The Times*

'This collection is surprisingly funny and compassionate. An invigorating book' *Marie Claire*

THINGS YOU SHOULD KNOW

A.M. Homes

GRANTA

Granta Publications, 12 Addison Avenue, London W11 4QR

First published in Great Britain by Granta Books 2003
Paperback edition published by Granta Books 2004
This edition published by Granta Books 2013

The following stories appeared originally in these publications:

"The Chinese Lesson": *Granta 74*
"Raft in Water, Floating": *New Yorker*, June 1999
"Rockets Round the Moon": *Writer's Harvest*, Harcourt Brace 1994
"Please Remain Calm": *Conjunctions*, May 2000
"Whiz Kids": *Christopher Street*, April 1992; also *Penguin Book of
Gay Fiction*, Viking 1994
"Do Not Disturb": *McSweeney's*, January 2000
"The Weather Outside is Sunny and Bright": *Rachel Whiteread
Catalogue*, Guggenheim, Berlin, 2000

A CIP catalogue record for this book is
available from the British Library.

1 3 5 7 9 10 8 6 4 2

ISBN 978-1-84708-729-4

Printed and bound by CPI Group (UK) Ltd, Croydon, CR0 4YY

In Memory of Robert S. Jones

CONTENTS

CONTENTS

ix

THE CHINESE LESSON

I am walking, holding a small screen, watching the green dot move like the blip of a plane, the blink of a ship's radar. Searching. I am on the lookout for submarines. I am an air traffic controller trying to keep everything at the right distance. I am lost.

A man steps out of the darkness onto the sidewalk. "Plane gone down?" he asks.

It is nearly night; the sky is still blue at the top, but it is dark down here.

"I was just walking the dog," he says.

I nod. The dog is nowhere to be seen.

"You're not from around here are you?"

"Not originally," I say. "But we're over on Maple now."

"Tierney," the man says. "John Tierney."

"Harris," I say. "Geordie Harris."

"Welcome to the neighborhood. Welcome to town."

He points to my screen; the dot seems to have stopped traveling.

"I was hoping to hell that was a toy—a remote control," he says. "I was hoping to have some fun. Are you driving a car or floating a boat somewhere around here?"

"It's a chip," I say, cutting him off. "A global positioning screen. I'm looking for my mother-in-law."

There is a scratching sound from inside a nearby privet, and the unmistakable scent of dog shit rises like smoke.

"Good boy," Tierney says. "He doesn't like to do his business in public. Can't blame him—if they had me shitting outside, I'd hide in the bushes too."

Tierney—I hear it like *tyranny*. Tyrant, teaser, taunting me about my tracking system, my lost mother-in-law.

"It's not a game," I say, looking down at the blinking green dot.

A yellow Lab pushes out of the bushes and Tierney clips the leash back onto his collar. "Let's go, boy," Tierney says, slapping the side of his leg. "Good luck," he calls, pulling the dog down the road.

The cell phone clipped to my belt rings. "Who was that?" Susan asks. "Was that someone you know?"

'It was a stranger, a total stranger, looking for a playmate." I glance down at the screen. "She doesn't seem to be moving now."

"Is your antenna up?" Susan asks.

There is a pause. I hear her talking to Kate. "See Daddy. See Daddy across the street, wave to Daddy. Kate's waving," she tells me. I stare across the road at the black Volvo idling by the curb. With my free hand I wave back.

"That's Daddy," Susan says, handing Kate the phone.

"What are you doing, Daddy?" Kate asks. Her intonation, her annoyance, oddly accusatory for a three-year-old.

"I'm looking for Grandma."

"Me too," Kate giggles.

"Give the phone to Mommy."

"I don't think so," Kate says.

"Bye, Kate."

"What's new?" Kate says—it's her latest phrase.

"Bye-bye," I say, hanging up on her.

I step off the sidewalk and dart between the houses, through the grass alley that separates one man's yard from another's. A sneak, a thief, a prowling trespasser, I pull my flashlight out of my jacket and flick it on. The narrow Ever-

Ready beam catches patios and planters and picnic tables by surprise. I am afraid to call out, to attract attention. Ahead of me there is a basketball court, a slide, a sandbox, and there she is, sailing through my beam like an apparition. Her black hair blowing, her hands smoothly clutching the chain-link ropes of the swing as though they were reins. I catch her in mid-flight. Legs swinging in and out. I hold the light on her—there and gone.

"I'm flying," she says, sailing through the night.

I step in close so that she has to stop swinging. "Did you have a pleasant flight, Mrs. Ha?"

"It was nice."

"Was there a movie?"

She eases herself off the swing and looks at me like I'm crazy. She looks down at the tracking device. "It's no game," Mrs. Ha says, putting her arm through mine. I lead her back through the woods. "What's for dinner, Georgie?" she says. And I hear the invisible echo of Susan's voice correcting—it's not Georgie, it's Geordie.

"What would you like, Mrs. Ha?"

In the distance, a fat man presses against a sliding glass door, looking out at us, his breath fogging the pane.

Susan is at the computer, drawing. She is making a map, a grid of the neighborhood. She is giving us something to go on in the future—coordinates.

She is an architect, everything is line, everything is order. Our house is G4. The blue light of the screen pours over her, pressing the flat planes of her face flatter still—illuminating. She hovers in an eerie blue glow.

"I called Ken," I say.

Ken is the one who had the chip put in. He is Susan's brother. When Mrs. Ha was sedated for a colonoscopy, Ken had the chip implanted at the bottom of her neck, above her shoulder blades. The chip company specialist came and stood by while a plastic surgeon inserted it just under the skin. Before they let her go home, they tested it by wheeling her gurney all over the hospital while Ken sat in the waiting room tracking her on the small screen.

"Why?"

"I called him about her memory. I was wondering if we should increase her medication."

Ken is a psychopharmacologist, a specialist in the containment of feeling. He used to be a stoner and now he is a shrink. He has no affect, no emotions.

"And?" she says.

"He asked if she seemed agitated."

"She seems perfectly happy," Susan says.

"I know," I say, not telling Susan what I told Ken—Susan is the one who's agitated.

"Does she know where she is?" Ken had asked. There had been a pause, a moment where I wondered if he was asking about Susan or his mother. "I'm not always sure," I'd said, failing to differentiate.

"Well, what did he say?" Susan wants to know.

"He said we could try upping the dose—no harm in trying. He said it's not unusual for old people to wander off at twilight, to forget where they are. He said there are all kinds of phenomena that no one really understands."

"You haven't ever called my brother before, have you?" Susan asks.

"I have not, no."

Mrs. Ha has only been with us for three weeks. Before that, she was in her own apartment in California, slowly evaporating. It was a fall that brought her to the hospital, a phone call to Ken, a series of tests, the chip implant, and then Ken put her on a plane to us—with a pair of tracking devices packed in her suitcase. When she arrived I drove her around the neighborhood, I showed her where the stores were, the library, post office, and the train station. I don't tell Susan that now I live in fear Mrs. Ha will find the station herself, that she'll hop on a train—and the mother hunt will become an FBI investigation. We have only been here ourselves for five months, before that we were on 106th and Riverside, and most mornings when I wake up I still have no idea where I am.

"I don't like coming home any more," Susan says, turning to face me, the light from the computer an iMac aura around her head. "It scares me. I never know what to expect." She pauses. "I can't do it."

"You can do it," I say, plucking a fragment from my childhood, the memory of Shari Lewis telling Lamb Chop, "You can do anything."

There is nothing Susan likes less than to fail. She will do anything not to fail; she will not try so as not to fail.

Susan is reading. She turns the pages of her book, neatly, tightly, they almost click as they flip. "Listen to this," she says, quoting a passage from *In Cold Blood.* "'Isn't it wonderful, Kansas is so American.'"

When I told my family about Susan, they said, "She doesn't sound Chinese."

"An architect named Susan from Yale who grew up in LaJolla—that's not Chinese," my mother said.

"But she is Chinese," I repeated.

And later when I told Susan the story she said angrily, "I'm not Chinese, I'm American."

Susan is minimal, flat, like Kansas. She is physically nonexistent, a plank of wood, planed, smooth. There is nothing to curl around, nothing to hold on to. Her design signature is a thin ledge, floating on a wall, a small trough wide enough to want to rest something on, too narrow to hold anything.

I drape my arm over her, it lies across her body like dead weight. Her exhalations blow the little hairs on my arm like a warm wind.

"You're squishing me," she says, pushing my arm away. She turns the page—click.

"When she dies do they take the chip out?" Susan asks, hooking me with her leg, pulling me back.

"I assume they just deactivate it and you give them back the tracker—it's leased."

"Should we have one put in Kate?"

"Let's see how it goes with your mother. No one knows if there are side effects, weird electromagnetic pulls toward outer space from being tracked, traced as you walk along the earth."

"Where did you find her tonight?" she asks as we are falling asleep. We sleep like plywood, pressed together—two straight lines.

"On a swing. How can you be angry with an old woman on a swing?"

"She's my mother."

In the morning Mrs. Ha is in the front yard. She is playing a Jimi Hendrix tape she brought with her on our boom box: she is a tree, a rock, a cloud. She is shifting slowly between poses, holding them, and then morphing into the next.

"T'ai chi," Susan says.

"I didn't know people really did that."

"They all do it," Susan says, glaring at me. "Even I can do it." She takes a couple of poses, the first like a vulture about to attack, her fingers suddenly talons, and then she is a dragon, hissing.

When Susan and I met there was a gap between us, a neutral space. I saw it as an acknowledgment of the unbridgeable, not just male and female, but unfamiliar worlds—we couldn't pretend to understand each other.

I look back out the window. Kate is there now, standing next to Mrs. Ha, doing her kung fu imitation chop-chops. Kate punches the air, she kicks. She has nothing on under her dress.

"Kate needs underpants," I tell Susan, who runs, horrified, down the stairs, shooing the two of them into the backyard.

For a moment the boom box is alone on the grass—Jimi Hendrix wailing "And the wind cries Mary," at 8:28 A.M.

I see Sherika, the nanny, coming up the sidewalk. Sherika takes the train from Queens every morning. "I could never live here," she told us the day we moved in. "I have to be around people." Sherika is a single ebony stick almost six feet tall. She moves like a gazelle, like she is gliding toward the house. In Uganda, where she grew up, her family is part of the royal family—she may even be a princess.

I go downstairs and open the door for her. My top half is dressed in shirt and tie, my bottom half still pajamaed.

"How are you doing this morning?" she asks, her intonation so melodious, each word so evenly enunciated that just the sound of her voice is a comfort.

"I'm fine, and you?"

"Good. Very good," she says. "Where are my ladies?"

"In the backyard, warming up." I am still standing in the hall. "What does the name Sherika mean?" I'm thinking it's something tribal, something mystical. I picture a tall bird with thin legs and an unusual sound.

"I have no idea," she says. "It's just what my auntie in Brooklyn calls me. My true name is Christine." She smiles. "Today, I am going to take my ladies to the library and then maybe I'll take my ladies out to lunch."

I find my wallet on the table and hand Christine forty dollars. "Take them to lunch," I say. "That would be nice."

"Thank you," she says, putting the money in her pocket.

Susan and I walk ourselves to the train, leaving the car for Sherika-Christine.

"Fall is here, clocks go back tomorrow, we can rake leaves this weekend," I say as we head down the sidewalk. It is my fantasy to spend Saturday in the yard, raking. "We have to give it a year."

"And then what—put her in a home?"

"I'm talking about the house—we have to give ourselves a

year to get used to the house." There is a pause, a giant black crow takes flight in front of us. "We need shades in the bedroom, the upstairs bathroom needs to be regrouted, it's all starting to annoy me."

"It can't be perfect."

"Why not?"

Sitting next to Susan on the train, I feel like I'm a foreigner, not just a person from another country but a person from another planet, a person without customs, ways of being, a person who has blank spots rather than bad habits. I am thinking about Susan, about what it means to be married to someone I know nothing about.

"It's exhausting," I say, "all this back and forth."

"It's eighteen minutes longer than coming down from 106th Street."

"It feels farther."

"It is farther," she says, "but you're moving faster." She turns the page.

"Do you ever wonder what I'm thinking?"

"I know what you're thinking, you confess every thought."

"Not every thought."

"Ninety-nine percent," she says.

"Does that bother you?"

"No," she says. "Everything is not so important, everything is not earth-shattering, despite what you think."

I am silenced.

We arrive at Grand Central. Susan puts her book in her bag and is off the train. "Call me," I say. Every morning when we separate there is a moment when I think I will never see her again. She disappears into the crowd, and I think that's it, it's over, that's all there was.

Twenty minutes later, I call her at the office—"Just making sure you got there OK."

"I'm here," she says.

"I want something," I confess.

"What do you want?"

"I don't know," I say. "More. I want more of something."

Connection, I am thinking. I want connection.

"You want something I don't have," she says.

I am at my desk, drifting, remembering the summer my parents divorced and my bar mitzvah was canceled due to lack of interest on all sides.

"I just can't imagine doing it," my mother said. "I can't imagine doing anything with your father, can you? I think it would be very uncomfortable."

My father gave me $5,000 to "make up the difference," then asked, "Is that enough?" I spent my thirteenth birthday with him in a New York hotel room, eating ice-cream cake from 31 Flavors with a woman whose name my father couldn't remember. "Tell my friend about school, tell my friend what you do for fun, tell my friend all about yourself," he kept saying, and all I wanted to do was scream—What the fuck is your friend's name?

On Memorial Day weekend, my mother married her "friend," Howard, and took off on an eight-week second honeymoon, and I was sent to my father's new townhouse condo in Philadelphia.

There was a small room for me, made out of what had been a walk-in closet. My father was taking cooking lessons, learning a thousand and one things to do with a wok. On different days, different women would come for dinner. "I'm living the good life," my father would tell me. "I'm getting all I want." I would eat dinner with my father and his date and then excuse myself and hide in my closet.

I spent my summer at the pool, living entirely in the water, with goggles, with fins. I fell in love with the bottom of the pool, a silky sky-blue, a slippery second skin. I spent days walking up and down, trying to figure the exact point where I could still have my feet on the ground and my head above water.

"It's vinyl," I heard the lifeguard tell someone.

The extreme stillness of the sky, the hot, oxygenless air, the water strong like bleach, was blinding, sterile, intoxicating, perfect.

The only other person who came to the pool regularly was a girl who had just been in the nuthouse for not eating. Deformedly thin, she would slather herself with lotion and lie out and bake. She was only allowed to swim one hour a day, and at noon her mother would carry out a tray and she had to eat everything on it—"or else I'm taking you back," her mother would say.

"Don't stand over me. Don't treat me like a baby."

"Don't act like a baby."

And then the mother would look at me. "Would you like half a sandwich?"

I'd nod and she'd give me half a sandwich, which I'd eat still standing in the water, goggles on, feet touching the bottom.

"See," the mother would say. "He eats. And not only does he eat, he doesn't make crumbs."

"He's in the water," the girl would say.

In the evening I would crawl into my cave and read postcards from my mother—*Venice is everything I thought it would be, France is stunning, London theater is so much better than Broadway. Thinking of you, hoping you're having a fantastic summer. I am imagining you swimming across America. Love Mom.*

"We're still your parents, we're just not together," became the new refrain.

Later, when I started to date, when I would go to girls' houses and their mothers and fathers would ask, "What do your parents do?" I'd say, "They're divorced," as though it were a full-time job. They'd look at me, instantly dismissive, as though I too was doomed to divorce, as though domestic instability was genetically passed down.

And then, later still, there were families I fell in love with.

I remember sitting at the Segals' dining room table, happily slurping chicken soup, looking up at Cindy Segal, who stood above me, bread basket in hand, glaring at me in disgust. "You're just another one of them," she said, dropping the bread, unceremoniously dumping me. Too stunned to swallow, I felt soup dribble down my chin.

"Don't go," Mrs. Segal said, as Cindy slammed upstairs to her room. After that, the Segals would sometimes call me. "Cindy's not going to be here," they'd say, "come visit." I went a couple of times and then Cindy joined a cult and never spoke to any of us again.

My mother used to say, marry someone familiar, marry someone you have something in common with. The flatness of Susan, the hollow, the absence of some unnameable something—was familiar. The sensation that she was on the outside, waiting to be invited in, was something we had in common.

Never did Susan ask for an accounting of my past, never did she pull back and say—"You're not going to hurt me, are you? You don't have any weird diseases, do you? You're not married, right?"

Susan looked at me once, squarely, evenly, and said, "Nice tie," and that was it.

In the morning, after our first night together, she rearranged my furniture. Everything immediately looked better.

It is late in the afternoon; I have spent the day lost in thought. There are contracts spread across my desk waiting for my review. Outside, it is getting dark. I leave and instinctively walk uptown. All day I have been thinking about the house, about Mrs. Ha, and now I am heading toward our old apartment as though it were all a dream. I am walking, looking forward to seeing the grocer on the corner, to riding up in the elevator with Willy, the elevator man, to smelling the neighbors' dinner cooking. I am thinking that once these things happen, I will feel better, returned to myself. I go three blocks before I catch myself and realize that I am moving in the wrong direction. I belong in Larchmont—Larchmont like Loch Ness. I hurry toward the station. Stepping onto the train, I have the feeling I am leaving something behind. I check my messages—Susan has left word, something about a client, something about something falling, something about it all being her fault, something about staying late. "I don't know when," she says, and then we are in a tunnel and the signal is lost.

I am going home. I imagine arriving at the house and having Sherika tell me Mrs. Ha is gone again. I picture changing into hunting clothes, a red-and-black wool jacket, an orange vest, a special hat, and going in search of her, carrying some kind of wooden whistle I have carved myself—a mother-in-law call. I imagine Mrs. Ha hearing the rolling rattle of my call *Mrs. Haa . . . Mrs. Haaa Haa . . . Mrs. Ha Ha Ha . . . Mrs. Haaaaaahhhh*—it ends in an upswing. She is roused from her dream state, her head tilts toward the sound of my whistle, and she is summoned home as mystically as she was called away.

I phone Sherika and ask—can she stay late, can she keep an extra eye on Mrs. Ha. I take a taxi from the train—there is the odd suburban phenomenon of the shared cab, strangers piling in, stuffing themselves into the back of the sedan, brief-cases held on laps like shields, and then each calls out his address and we are off on a madcap ride, the driver tearing down the streets, whipping around corners, depositing us at our doorsteps for seven dollars a head.

Home. The sky is five minutes from dark, the floodlights are already on in the backyard. Kate and Mrs. Ha are down in the dirt, squatting, elbows resting on thighs, buttocks dropped down, positioned as if about to shit.

"Mrs. Ha, what are you doing?"

"I am thinking, Georgie. And I am resting."

There is something frightening about it—Kate imitating Mrs. Ha, grotesque in her gestures, rubber-limbed like a circus clown, contorting herself for attention, more alive than I will ever be. Her freedom, her full expression terrifying me—I am torn between interrupting and simply watching her be.

"We are planting a garden," Sherika says, straightening up, extending to her full six feet. "After lunch I took them to the nursery. We are putting in bulbs for spring."

"Tulips," Kate says.

Sherika drops sixty-nine cents of change into my hand and somehow I feel guilty, like I should have left her a hundred dollars or my credit card.

"What a good idea," I say.

"We are just finishing up. Come on, ladies, let's go inside and wash our hands."

I follow them into the kitchen. They wash their hands and then look at me, as though I should have something in mind, a plan for what happens next.

"Let's go for a ride," I say, unable to bear the anxiety of staying home. Not knowing where else to go, I drive them to the supermarket. Sherika takes Mrs. Ha and I have Kate and we go up and down the aisles, filling the cart.

"Are you the apple of your daddy's eye?" A clerk in the produce section pulls Kate's hair and then looks at me. "There's lots of these Chinese babies now, nobody wants them so they give them away. My wife's sister adopted one—otherwise they drown 'em like kittens. You don't want to be drowned, do you, sweetheart," he says, looking at Kate again.

"She's not adopted. She's mine."

"Oh sorry," the guy says, flustered as though he'd said something even more insulting than what he actually said. "I'm really sorry." He backs away.

Sorry about what? I look at Kate. Her head is too big. Her

skin is an odd jaundicy yellow and now she's playing some weird game with the cantaloupes, banging them against the floor. It occurs to me that the guy thought there was something wrong with her.

"Did you find everything you were looking for?" Sherika asks as we're wheeling up the frozen foods toward the checkout.

"I'm finished."

In a strip mall across the street, I notice an Asian grocery store. When the light changes, I pull in.

"Ah," Sherika says, "look at that."

It is small, dingy, and a little otherworldly. There are wire racks for shelves, and things floating in tubs filled with melting ice—none of it incredibly clean. Mrs. Ha scurries around collecting tins of spices, bottles of vinegar. She seems happy, like she has recovered herself, she is chatting with the man behind the counter.

She shows me fresh vegetables: water chestnuts, shanghai cabbage, *"Bau dau gok,"* she says,—"snake bean." Lotus leaves, brown slab sugar, and now she is in the freezer case, handing me a bag that says FROZEN FISH BALLS. She hands me others with writing in Chinese. *"Fatt choy?"* she asks the man behind the counter, and he points toward it.

"What is it?" I ask.

"Black moss," she says.

"What is it really?" I ask.

She shrugs.

I want Mrs. Ha to feel comfortable. If pressed seaweed is to her what mashed potatoes are to me, I want her to have ten packages. Why not? I start picking things off the shelf and offering them to her.

She shakes her head and continues shopping.

The man behind the counter says something and she laughs; I am sure it is about me. I hear something about three

Georges, about water, and then a lot of clucking from Mrs. Ha. He talks quickly, flipping back and forth from Chinese to broken English. She answers—her speech, suddenly rhythmic, her accent shifting into the pure diphthong, the *oo* long, an ancient incantation.

The man takes a small beautiful box out from a shelf below the counter. Mrs. Ha makes a soft cooing sound before he opens it. "Bird's nest," he says. "Very good quality."

"What is bird's nest?"

The man blows spit bubbles at me. He drools intentionally and then sucks his saliva back in. "The spit of a swift," he says, flapping his arms.

Mrs. Ha checks her pockets for money, finds nothing, and looks at me as if to ask, Can we get it?

"Sure, why not?"

"I have never had so much home in a long time," she says.

"Come again soon," the man says, as we are leaving. "Play bingo."

I carry two shopping bags out to the car, imagining Mrs. Ha is going to start dating this man—I picture tracking twin positioning chips, two dots, one on top of the other. I make a mental note to ask Susan—is Mrs. Ha allowed to date?

In the car on the way home Mrs. Ha asks, "Do you like Sony? Mr. Sony make the tape recorder and Mr. Nixon make friends with the Chinese. Then Mr. Nixon erase and now Mr. Sony die, I read in your *New York Times*." She laughs. "Stupid old men."

Kate is on the floor in front of the television. Mrs. Ha is in the kitchen making soup. Sherika takes the car to the train station; she will drop it off and go home to Queens, Susan will pick it up and come home to us.

"What's that smell?" Susan says when she comes in the door.

"Your mother is making soup."

"It's so weirdly familiar, I thought I was hallucinating."

"Everything OK?" I am looking at her, trying to tell if she is lying, if there's more to the story or not.

"It's fine," she says. "It's fine. He got hysterical, a little piece of the wall came down—it wasn't my fault. I was so upset. I thought I had done something wrong."

I don't tell Susan that I was worried she might not come back. I don't tell her that I took everyone to the supermarket because the idea of staying alone in the house with the three of them inexplicably terrified me.

"Dinner is ready," Mrs. Ha says.

"It looks delicious." I stare into my bowl. There are white things and black things floating in the soup—nothing recognizable. I am starving. I assume it is mushrooms.

"Hot," Kate says, her face over the bowl, blowing steam like a dragon.

Susan stares speechless at her bowl.

The broth is rich, succulent. I slurp. It is skin, skin and bones, small bones, soft, like little fingers, melting in the mouth.

I look at Susan. "Feet?" I ask in Latin. Susan nods.

I don't want to say anything more. I don't want to throw Kate off—she is eating, not noticing. And Mrs. Ha is clearly enjoying herself.

"Georgie took me shopping," Mrs. Ha says.

"I had a late lunch." Susan carries her bowl into the kitchen.

Later, I overhear her on the phone with her brother, whispering. "She tried to poison me, she made chicken-feet soup."

I pick up the extension in the kitchen and hope neither of them notices the click.

"Where did she get the feet?"

"I think he's helping her."

"Who?"

"Geordie."

"Why?"

"He hates me."

I hang up.

When I was young my mother made cupcakes for my birthday and brought them to school. The teacher had us all write her thank-you notes in thick pencil on wide-lined paper. *Dear Mrs. Harris, thank you for the delicious cupcakes. We enjoyed them very much. Sincerely, Geordie.*

"Dear Mrs. Harris, Sincerely Geordie, what kind of letter is that to send a mother?" She still talks about how funny it was. When she telephones and I answer she says, "It's Mrs. Harris, your mother."

We are in bed. Susan is reading. I look over her shoulder, page 297 of *In Cold Blood,* a description of Perry Smith, one of the murderers. "He seems to have grown up without direction, without love."

"I'm lonely," I tell her.

"Read something," she says, turning the page.

I go downstairs and fix a bowl of ice cream for Susan.

"I'm not your enemy," I tell her when the ice cream is gone, when I have helped her finish it, when I am licking the bowl.

"I don't know that," she says, taking the bowl away from me and putting it on the floor. "You act like you're on her side."

"And what side is that?"

"The side of the dead, of things past."

"Oh, please," I say, and yet there is something in what Susan is saying; I am on the side of things lost, I am in the past, remembering. "You're scaring me," I say. "You're turning into some weird minimalist monster from hell."

"This is me," Susan says. "This is my life. You're intruding."

"This is our family," I say, horrified.

"I can't be Chinese," Susan tells me. "I've spent my whole life trying not to be Chinese."

"Kate is half Chinese and she likes it," I say, trying to make Susan feel better.

"I don't like that half of Kate," Susan says.

Something summons me from my sleep. I listen—on alert, heart racing. The extreme silence of night is blasting full volume. Moon pours into the room like a gigantic night light. Outside, the trees are still—it is haunting, romantic, deeply autumnal. Night.

And there it is, far away, catching me, a kind of bleating, a baleful wail.

I go down the hall, each step amplified, the quieter I try to go the louder I become.

I check Kate—she is fast asleep.

It becomes more of a moan—deep, inconsolable, hollow. There is no echo, each beatified bellow is here and then gone, evaporating into the night.

Downstairs, Mrs. Ha is crouched in the corner of the living room, like a new end table. She is next to the sofa, squatting, her hands at her ears, crying. She is naked.

"Mrs. Ha?"

She doesn't answer.

Her cry, heartbreaking, definitive, filled with horror, with grief, with fear, comes from someplace far away, from somewhere long ago.

I touch her shoulder. "It's Geordie. Is there something I can do? Are you all right?"

I step on the foot switch for the lamp; the halogen torch floods the room. Susan's Corbusier chairs sit bolt upright—tight black leather boxes, a Prouve table from France lies flat, waiting, the modernist edge, dissonant, vibrating against the Tudor, the stone, the old casement windows, and Mrs. Ha, my Chinese mother-in-law, sobbing at my feet. I turn the light off.

"Mrs. Ha?" I lift her up, I put my hands under her arms and pull. She is compact like a panda, she is made of heavy metal. Her skin is at once papery thin and thick like hide. She clings to me, digging in.

I carry her back to her bed. She cries. I find her nightgown and slip it over her head. When she cries, her mouth drops open, her lips roll back, her chin tilts up and her teeth and jaws flash, like a horse's head. It is as though someone has just told her the most horrible thing; her face contorts. Her expression is like an anthropological find—at eighty-nine she is a living skeleton.

I touch her hair.

"I want to go home," she wails.

"You are home."

"I want to go home," she repeats.

I sit on the edge of her bed, I put my arms around her. "Maybe it was the soup, maybe the dinner didn't agree with you."

"No," she says, "I always have the soup. It is not the soup that does not agree with me, it is me that does not agree with me." She stops crying. "They are going to flood my home, I read it in the *New York Times,* they build the three gorges, the dam, and everything goes underwater."

"I don't know who they are," I say.

"You are who they are," she says. I don't know what she is talking about.

Mrs. Ha reaches to scratch her back, between her shoulder blades. "There is something there," she says. "I just can't reach it."

I imagine the little green blip on the tracking device, wobbling. "It's OK. Everything is all right now."

"You have no idea," she tells me as she is drifting off. "I am an old woman but I am not stupid."

And when she is asleep, I go back to bed. I am drenched in sweat. Susan turns toward me. "Everything all right?"

"Mrs. Ha was crying."

"Don't call her Mrs. Ha."

I take off my shirt, thinking I must smell like Mrs. Ha. I

smell like Mrs. Ha and sweat and fear. "What would you like me to call her—Ma Ha?"

"She has a name," Susan says angrily. "Call her Lillian."

I cannot sleep. I am thinking we have to take Mrs. Ha home. I am imagining a family trip reuniting Mrs. Ha with her country, Susan with her roots, Kate with her ancestry. I am thinking that I need to know more. I once read a story in a travel magazine about a man who went on a bike ride in China. I pictured a long open road, a rural landscape. In the story the man falls off his bike, breaks his hip, and lies on the side of the road until he realizes no help is going to come, and then he fashions his broken bike into a cane, raises himself up, and hobbles back to town.

RAFT IN WATER, FLOATING

She is lying on a raft in water. Floating. Every day when she comes home from school, she puts on her bikini and lies in the pool—it stops her from snacking.

"Appearances are everything," she tells him when he comes crashing through the foliage, arriving at the edge of the yard in his combat pants, thorns stuck to his shirt.

"Next time they change the code to the service gate, remember to tell me," he says. "I had to come in through the Eisenstadts' and under the wire."

He blots his face with the sleeve of his shirt. "There's some sort of warning—I can't remember if it's heat or air."

"I might evaporate," she says, then pauses. "I might spontaneously combust. Do you ever worry about things like that?"

"You can't explode in water," he says.

Her raft drifts to the edge.

He sits by the side of the pool, leaning over, his nose pressed into her belly, sniffing. "You smell like swimming. You smell clean, you smell white, like bleach. When I smell you, my nostrils dilate, my eyes open."

"Take off your shirt," she says.

"I'm not wearing any sunblock," he says.

"Take off your shirt."

He does, pulling it over his head, flashing twin woolly birds' nests under his arms.

He rocks her raft. His combat pants tent. He puts one hand inside her bathing suit and the other down his pants.

She stares at him.

He closes his eyes, his lashes flicker. When he's done, he dips his hand in the pool, splashing it back and forth as though checking the water, taking the temperature. He wipes it on his pants.

"Do you like me for who I am?" she asks.

"Do you want something to eat?" he replies.

"Help yourself."

He gets cookies for himself and a bowl of baby carrots from the fridge for her. The bowl is cold, clear glass, filled with orange stumps. "Butt plugs," he calls them.

The raft is a silver tray, a reflective surface—it holds the heat.

"Do you have any idea what's eating me?"

"You're eating yourself," he says.

A chunk of a Chips Ahoy! falls into the water. It sinks.

She pulls on her snorkel and mask and stares at the sky. The sound of her breath through the tube is amplified, a raspy, watery gurgle. "Mallory, my malady, you are my Mallomar, my favorite cookie," he intones. "Chocolate-dipped, squishy . . . You were made for me."

She flips off the raft and into the water. She swims.

"I'm going," she hears him say. "Going, going, gone."

At twilight an odd electrical surge causes the doorbells all up and down the block to ring. An intercom chorus of faceless voices sings a round of "Hi, hello. Can I help you? Is anybody out there?"

She climbs out of the pool, wet feet padding across the flagstone. Behind her is a Japanese rock garden, a retaining wall holding the earth in place like a restraining order. She sits on the warm stones. Dripping. Watering the rocks. In school, when she was little, she was given a can of water and a paintbrush—she remembers painting the playground fence, watching it turn dark and then light again as the water evaporated.

She watches her footprints disappear.

The dog comes out of the house. He puts his nose in her crotch. "Exactly who do you think you are?" she asks, pushing him away.

There is the outline of hills in the distance; they are perched on a cliff, always in danger of falling, breaking away, sliding.

Inside, there is a noise, a flash of light.

"Shit!" her mother yells.

She gets up. She opens the sliding glass door. "What happened?"

"I flicked the switch and the bulb blew."

She steps inside—cool white, goose bumps.

"I dropped the plant," her mother says. She has dropped an African violet on its head. "I couldn't see where I was going." She has a blue gel pack strapped to her face. "Headache."

There is dark soil on the carpet. She goes to get the Dustbuster. The television in the kitchen is on, even though no one is watching: "People often have the feeling there is something wrong, that they are not where they should be. . . ."

The dirt is in a small heap, a tiny hill on the powder-blue carpet. In her white crocheted bathing suit, she gets down on her hands and knees and sucks it up. Her mother watches. And then her mother gets down and brushes the carpet back and forth. "Did you get it?" she asks. "Did you get it all?"

"All gone," she says.

"I dropped it on its head," her mother says. "I can't bear it. I need to be reminded of beauty," she says. "Beauty is a comfort, a reminder that good things are possible. And I killed it."

"It's not dead," she says. "It's just upside down." Her mother is tall, like a long thin line, like a root going down.

In the front yard they hear men speaking Spanish, the sound of hedge trimmers and weed whackers, frantic scratching, a thousand long fingernails clawing to get in.

There is the feeling of a great divide: us and them. They rely on the cleaning lady and her son to bring them things—her mother claims to have forgotten how to grocery-shop. All they can do is open the refrigerator door and hope there is something inside. They live on the surface in some strange state of siege.

They are standing in the hallway outside her sister's bedroom door.

"You don't own me," her sister says.

"Believe me, I wouldn't want to," a male voice says.

"And why not, aren't I good enough?" her sister says.

"Is she fighting with him again?"

"On speakerphone," her mother says. "I can't tell which one is which, they all sound the same." She knocks on the door. "Did you take your medication, Julie?"

"You are in my way," her sister says, talking louder now.

"What do you want to do about dinner?" her mother asks. "Your father is late—can you wait?"

"I had carrots."

She goes into her parents' room and checks herself in the bathroom mirror—still there. Her eyes are green, her lips are chapped pink. Her skin is dry from the chlorine, a little irritated. She turns around and looks over her shoulder—she is pruny in the back, from lying on the wet raft.

She opens the cabinet—jars, tubes, throat cream and thigh cream, lotion, potion, bronze stick, cover-up, pancake, base. She piles it on.

"Make sure you get enough water—it's hot today," her mother says. Her parents have one of those beds where each half does a different thing; right now her father's side is up, bent in two places. They both want what they want, they need what they need. Her mother is lying flat on her face.

She goes back out to the pool. She dives in with a splash. Her mother's potions run off, forming an oil slick around her.

Her father comes home. Through the glass she sees the

front door open. She sees him moving from room to room. "Is the air filter on?" His voice is muffled. "Is the air on?" he repeats. "I'm having it again—the not breathing."

He turns on the bedroom light. It throws her parents into relief; the sliding glass doors are lit like a movie screen. IMAX Mom and Dad. She watches him unbutton his shirt. "I'm sweating," she hears him say. Even from where she is, she can see that he is wet. Her father calls his sweat "proof of his suffering." Under his shirt, a silk T-shirt is plastered to his body, the dark mat of the hair on his back showing through. There is something obscene about it—like an ape trying to look human. There is something embarrassing about it as well—it looks like lingerie, it makes him look more than naked. She feels as if she were seeing something she shouldn't, something too personal.

Her mother rolls over and sits up.

"Something is not right," he says.

"It's the season," she says.

"Unseasonable," he says. "Ben got a call in the middle of the afternoon. They said his house was going downhill fast. He had to leave early."

"It's an unpredictable place," her mother says.

"It's not the same as it was, that's the thing," her father says, putting on a dry shirt. "Now it's a place where everybody thinks he's somebody and nobody wants to be left out."

She gets out of the pool and goes to the door, pressing her face against the glass. They don't notice her. Finally, she knocks. Her father opens the sliding glass door. "I didn't see you out there," he says.

"I'm invisible," she says. "Welcome home."

She is back in the pool. Floating. The night is moist. Vaporous. It's hard to know if it's been raining or if the sprinkler system is acting up. The sky is charcoal, powdery black. Everything is a little fuzzy around the edges but sharp and clear in the center.

There is a coyote at the edge of the grass. She feels it staring at her. "What?" she says.

It lowers its head and pushes its neck forward, red eyes like red lights.

"What do you want?"

The coyote's legs grow long, its fur turns into an overcoat, it stands, its muzzle melts into a face—an old woman, smiling.

"Who are you?" the girl asks. "Are you friends with my sister?"

"Watch me," the old woman says. She throws off the coyote coat—she is taller, she is younger, she is naked, and then she is a man.

She hears her mother and father in the house. Shouting.

"What am I to you?" her mother says.

"It's the same thing, always the same thing, blah, blah, blah," her father says.

"Have you got anything to eat?" the coyote asks.

"Would you like a carrot?"

"I was thinking of something more like a sandwich or a slice of cheese pizza."

"There are probably some waffles in the freezer. No one ever eats the waffles. Would you like me to make you one?"

"With butter and syrup?" he asks.

The girl nods.

He licks his lips, he turns his head and licks his shoulder and then his coyote paws. He begins grooming himself.

"Be right back," she says. She goes into the kitchen, opens the freezer, and pulls out the box of waffles.

"I thought you were on a diet," her mother says.

"I am," the girl says, putting the waffles in the toaster, getting the butter, slicing a few strawberries.

"What's this called, breakfast for dinner?"

"Never mind," the girl says, pouring syrup.

"That's all you ever say."

She goes back outside. A naked young woman sits by the edge of the pool.

"Is it still you?" the girl asks.

"Yes," the coyote says.

She hands the coyote the plate. "Usually we have better choices, but the housekeeper is on vacation."

"Yum, Eggos. Want a bite?"

The girl shakes her head. "I'm on a diet," she says, getting back onto her raft.

The coyote eats. When she's finished she licks the plate. Her tongue is incredibly long, it stretches out and out and out, lizardly licking.

"Delish," she says.

The girl watches, eyes bulging at the sight of the tongue—hot pink. The coyote starts to change again, to shift. Her skin goes dark, it goes tan, deep like honey and then crisper brown, as if it is burning, and then darker still, toward black. Downy feathers start to appear, and then longer feathers, like quills. Her feet turn orange, fold in, and web. A duck, a big black duck, like a dog, but a duck. The duck jumps into the pool and paddles toward the girl, splashing noisily.

"These feet," she says. "They're the opposite of high heels and still they're so hard to control."

They float in silence.

She sees her sister come out of her room. She watches the three of them, her mother, father, and sister, through the glass.

She floats on the raft.

Relaxed, the duck extends her neck, her feathers bleach white, and she turns into a swan, circling gracefully.

Suddenly, she lifts her head, as if alerted. She pumps her wings. Her body is changing again, she is trading her feathers for fur, a black mask appears around her eyes, her bill becomes a snout. She is out of the water, standing on the flagstone, a raccoon with orange webbed feet. She waddles off into the night.

27

Below ground there is a shift, a fissure, a crack that ricochets. A tremor. The house lights flicker. The alarm goes off. In the pool the water rolls, a small domestic tidal wave sweeps from one end to the other, splashing onto the stones.

The sliding glass door opens, her father steps out, flashlight circling the water. He finds her holding onto the ladder.

"You all right?" he asks.

"Fine," she says.

"Come on out now," he says. "It's enough for one day. You're a growing girl—you need your beauty sleep."

She climbs out of the pool.

Her father hands her a towel. "It's a wonder you don't just shrivel up and disappear."

GEORGICA

A phosphorescent dream. Everything hidden under cover of night becomes abundantly clear, luminescent.

Hiding in the dunes, she is a foot soldier, a spy, a lusty intruder. The sand caves in around her, the silky skin of another planet.

What was so familiar by day is inside out, an X ray etched in memory. The sands of Main Beach are foreign shores. With her night-vision goggles she scans the horizon on the lookout. At first there is just the moon on the water, the white curl of the waves, the glow of the bathhouse, the bleached aura of the parking lot. Far down the beach Tiki torches light figures dancing, ancient apparitions in a tribal meeting. Closer, there is a flash, the flick of a match, a father and daughter burst out of the darkness holding sparklers. They have come to the sea to set the world afire; thousands of miniature explosions erupt like anti-aircraft fire.

"More," the little girl shouts when the sparkler is done. "More."

"Do you think Mommy is home yet?" the father asks, lighting another one.

Checking her watch, she feels the pressure of time; the window of opportunity is small, twelve to twenty-four hours. Ready and waiting; her supplies are in a fanny pack around her waist, the car is parked under a tree at the far edge of the lot.

She has been watching them for weeks, watching without realizing she was watching, watching mesmerized, not thinking they might mean something to her, they might be useful. Tall, thin, with smooth muscled chests, hips narrow, shoulders square; they are growing, thickening, pushing out. Agile and lithe, they carry themselves with the casualness of young men, with the grace that comes from attention, from being noticed. These are hardworking boys, summer-job boys, scholarship boys, clean-cut boys, good boys, local boys, stunningly boyish boys, boys of summer, boys who every morning raise the American flag and every evening lower it, folding it carefully, beautiful boys. Golden boys. Like toasted Wonder Bread; she imagines they are warm to the touch.

She checks to be sure the coast is clear and then crosses to the tall white wooden tower, a steeple at the church of the sea.

She climbs. This is where they perch, ever ready to pull someone from the riptide, where they stand slapping red flags through the air, signaling, where they blow the whistle, summoning swimmers back to shore. "Ahoy there, you've gone too far."

She puts out supplies, stuffing condoms into the drink holders. She suspects they think the town is providing them as a service of some sort; she waits to read an angry letter to the editor, but no one says anything and they are always gone, pocketed, slipped into wallets, a dozen a day.

Carefully, she climbs back down the ladder and repositions herself in the sand. As she crawls forward, the damp sand rubs her belly, it slips under the elastic waistband of her pants and down her legs, tickling.

It began accidentally; fragments, seemingly unconnected, lodged in her thoughts, each leading to something new, each propelling her forward. At cocktail parties, in the grocery store, the liquor store, the hardware, the library, she was looking, thinking she would find someone, looking and seeing only pot bellies, bad manners, stupidity. She was looking for something else and instead she found them. She was looking without realizing she was looking. She had been watching for weeks before it occurred to her. An anonymous observer under the cover of summer, she spent her days sitting downwind, listening to their conversations. They talked about nothing—waves and water, movies, surfing, their parents and school, girls, hamburgers.

She found herself imagining luring one home. She imagined asking for a favor—could you change a bulb?—but worried it would seem too obvious.

She could picture the whole scenario: the boy comes to her house, she shows him the light, he stands on a chair, she looks up at his downy belly, at the bulge in his shorts, she hands him the bulb, brushing against him, she runs a hand up his leg, squeezing, tugging at his Velcro fly, releasing him.

They have a mythology all their own.

She caught herself enjoying the thought—it was the first time she'd allowed herself to think that way in months.

Now, she catches herself distracted, she puts her goggles back in place, she focuses. A cool wind is blowing the dune grass, sand skims through the air, biting, stinging, debriding.

A late-night fortune hunter emerges from the darkness, creeping across the parking lot, metal detector in hand. He shuffles onto the beach, sweeping for trinkets, looking for gold, listening on his headphones for the tick-tock of Timex, of Rolex. When he gets the signal he stops and with his homemade sifter scoops the sand, sifting it like flour, pocketing loose change.

She hears them approaching, the blast of a car radio, the bass beat a kind of early announcement of their arrival. Rock and roll. A truck pulls into the parking lot, they tumble out. This is home plate. Every morning, every night, they return, touching base, safe. Another car pulls in and then another. Traveling in packs, gangs, entourages, they spill onto the sand. And as if they know she is out there, they put on a show, piling high into a human pyramid. Laughing, they fall. One of the boys moons the others.

"Are you flashing or farting?"

Pawing at the sand with their feet, they wait to figure out what comes next.

There is something innocent and uncomplicated about them, an awkwardness she finds charming, adolescent arrogance that comes from knowing nothing about anything, not yet failing.

"We could go to my house, there's frozen pizza."

"We could get ice cream."

"There's a bonfire at Ditch Plains."

They piss on the dunes and are off again, leaving one behind—"See ya."

"Tomorrow," he says.

The one they've left sits on the steps of the bathhouse, waiting. He is one of them—she has seen him before, recognizes the tattoo, full circle around his upper arm, a hieroglyph. She has noticed how he wears his regulation red trunks long and low, resting on the top of his ass, a delicate tuft of hair poking up.

A white car pulls into the lot. A girl gets out. The light from the parking lot, combined with the humidity of the sea, fills the air with a humid glow that surrounds them like clouds. They stand, two angelic figures caught in her crosshairs. They walk hand in hand down to the beach. She trails after them, keeping a safe distance.

The night-vision glasses, enormously helpful, were not part of her original scenario. She bought them last weekend at a yard sale, at the home of a retired colonel. "They were mine, that's the original box," the colonel's son said, coming up behind her. "My father gave them to me for Christmas, they were crazy expensive. I think he wanted them for himself."

"Is there some way I can try them?"

He led her into his basement, pulling the door closed behind them. "I hope I'm not frightening you."

"I'm fine," she said.

"We unwrapped on Christmas Eve, my father turned off all the lights and made me try. I remember looking at the Christmas tree, weaving around the room, watching the lights move and then tripping, going down hard, and starting the new year with two black eyes like a raccoon."

"May I?"

He handed her the glasses, she reached out, feeling her way forward, their hands bumped. There was something terrifying about this unfamiliar dark; she stared at the glowing fish tank for comfort.

"The ON button is between the eyes." She flipped them on and suddenly she saw everything—ice skates, an old rowing machine, odd military memorabilia, a leaf blower, hammers and saws hanging from pegs. She saw everything and thought that in a minute she was going to see something extra, something she shouldn't see, a body in a clear plastic bag, slumped in the corner, a head on a stick, something unforgivably horrible. Everything had the eerie neon green of a horror movie, of information captured surreptitiously.

"If you're interested I'd be happy to throw in a bayonet and a helmet," he said, handing her one of each.

The boy and his girl are on the sand, making out. There is something delicate, tentative, in how they approach each other. Kissing and then pulling back, checking to see if it's okay, discovering how it feels, a tongue in the mouth, a hand on the breast, the press of a cock against the thigh.

He lifts her shirt, exposing an old-fashioned white bra. She unhooks it for him. Her breasts are surprisingly large, his hands are on them, not entirely sure what one does, his lack of skill endearing.

She feels the urgency of their desire. Without warning she finds herself excited.

He takes his sweatshirt off and lays it on the sand. They are one atop the other. She imagines the smell of him, suntan lotion, sweat, and sand, she imagines the smell of her—guacamole, fried onions, barbecue, stale cologne. She works either in a local restaurant or as a baby-sitter: formula, vomit, sour milk, stale cologne.

He rises for a minute, unzips his pants. His erection, long and lean, throbs in the moonlight. The girl takes it in her mouth. The boy kneels frozen, paralyzed by sensation, while the girl bobs up and down, like one of those trick birds drinking from a water glass.

She becomes alarmed, hopes they don't keep at it, not wanting to waste her shot.

"The condom, put on the condom," she is thinking out loud.

And then, finally, he pulls away, falls back on the sand, reaches into his pocket, locating it. He has trouble rolling it on—the girl helps. And then the girl is upon him, riding him, her bazoombas bouncing, floating like dirigibles. The boy lies back flattened, devastated, his arms straight up, reaching.

As soon as the condom is on, she feels her body opening. As soon as the girl is upon him, she is upon herself, warming to the touch. She wants to be ready. She is watching them and working herself. This is better than anything, more romantic, more relaxing than actually doing it with someone.

It ends abruptly. When they are done they are embarrassed, overwhelmed, suddenly strangers. They scramble for their clothing, hurry to the car, and are gone—into the night.

She waits until the coast is clear and then rushes toward the spot, finds it, and switches on her other light, a head-mounted work light, like a miner's lamp. She plucks the condom from the sand, holding the latex sheath of lust, of desire, carefully. The contents have not spilled, that's the good news, and he has performed well—the tip is full, she figures it's three or four cc. Working quickly, she pulls a syringe—no needle—from her fanny pack and lowers it into the condom. She has practiced this procedure at home using lubricated

Trojans and a combination of mayonnaise and Palmolive dish detergent. With one hand, she pulls back on the plunger, sucking it up. Holding the syringe upright, capping it, taking care not to lose any, she turns off her lights and makes a bee-line back up the beach to her car.

She has tilted the driver's seat back as far as it goes, and put a small pillow at the head end for her neck—she always has to be careful of the neck.

She gets into the car and puts herself in position, lying back, feet on the dash, hips tilted high. She is upside down like an astronaut prepared to launch, a modified yoga inversion, a sort of shoulder stand, more pillows under her hips, lifting her. The steering wheel helps hold her in place.

She is wearing sex pants. She has taken a seam ripper and opened the crotch, making a convenient yet private entry. She slips the syringe through the hole. When she's in as far as she can go, she pushes the plunger down—blastoff.

Closing her eyes, she imagines the sperm, stunned, drunken, in a whirl, ejaculated from his body into the condom and then out of the condom into her, swimming all the while. She imagines herself as part of their romance.

After a few minutes, she takes a sponge—wrapped in plastic, tied with a string—and pushes it in holding the sperm against her cervix.

Meditation. Sperm swimming, beach sperm, tadpole sperm, baby-whale sperm, boy sperm, millions of sperm. Sperm and egg. The egg launching, meeting the sperm in the fallopian tube, like the boy and girl meeting in the parking lot, coupling, traveling together, dividing, replicating, digging in, implanting.

She has been there about five minutes when there is a knock at the window, the beam of a flashlight looking in. She can't put down the window, because the ignition is off, she doesn't want to sit up, because it will ruin everything— she uses her left hand to open the car door.

"Yes?"

"Sorry to bother you, but you can't sleep here," the police officer says.

"I'm not sleeping, I'm resting."

The officer sees the pillows, he sees the soft collar around her neck—under the dim glow of the interior light, he sees her.

"Oh," he says. "It's you, the girl from last summer, the girl with the halo."

"That's me."

"Wow. It's good to see you up and around. Are you up and around? Is everything all right?"

"Fine," she says. "But I have these moments where I just have to lie down right then and there."

"Do you need anything? I have a blanket in the back of the car."

"I'll be all right, thank you."

He hangs around, standing just inside the car door, hands on his hips. "I was one of the first ones at the scene of the accident," he says. "I closed down the road when they took you over to the church—it was me with the flares who directed the helicopter in."

"Thank you," she says.

"I was worried you were a goner. People said they saw you fly through the air like a cannonball. They said they'd never seen anything like it."

"Umm," she says.

"I heard you postponed the wedding," he says.

"Canceled it."

"I can understand, given the circumstances."

She is waiting for him to leave.

"So, when you get like that, how long do you stay upside down?"

"About a half hour," she says.

"And how long has it been?"

"I'd say about fifteen minutes."

"Would you like to get a cup of coffee when you're done?"

"Aren't you on duty?"

"I could say I was escorting you home."

"Not tonight, but thanks."

"Some other time?"

"Sure."

"Sorry to hear about your grandmother—I read the obituary."

She nods. A couple of months ago, just after her ninety-eighth birthday, her grandmother died in her sleep—as graceful as it gets.

"That's a lot for one year—an accident, a canceled wedding, your grandmother passing."

"It is a lot," she says.

"You a birder?" he asks. "I see you've got binocs in the back seat."

"Always on the lookout," she says.

In a way she could see going for coffee, she could see marrying the local cop. He's not like a real cop, not someone you're going to worry isn't going to make it home at night. Out here she'd worry that he'd do something stupid—scurry up a telephone pole for a stuck cat.

He's still standing in the door.

"I guess I'd better go," he says, moving to close the car door. "I don't want to wear your battery down." He points at the interior light.

"Thanks again," she says.

"See you," he says, closing the door. He taps on the glass. "Drive carefully," he says.

She stays the way she is for a while longer and then pulls the pillows out from under, carefully unfolds herself, brings the seat back up, and starts the engine.

She drives home past the pond, there is no escaping it.

*   *   *

He was drunk. After a party he was always drunk.

"I'm drunk," he'd say going back for another.

"I'm drunk," he'd say when they'd said their good-byes and were walking down the gravel driveway in the dark.

"I'll drive," she'd say.

"It's my car," he'd say.

"You're drunk."

"Not really, I'm faking it."

An old Mercedes convertible. It should have been perfect, riding home with the top down in the night air, taken by the sounds of frogs, the crickets, Miles Davis on the radio, a million stars overhead, the stripe of the Milky Way, no longer worrying what the wind was doing to her hair—the party over.

It should have been perfect, but the minute they were alone there was tension. She disappeared, mentally, slipping back into the party, the clinking of glasses, bare-armed, bare-backed women, men sporty and tan, having gotten up early and taken the kids out for doughnuts, having spent the afternoon in action; tennis, golf, sailing, having had a nice long hot shower and a drink as they dressed for evening.

"Looking forward to planning a wedding?" one of the women had asked.

"No." She had no interest in planning a wedding. She was expected to marry him, but the more time that passed, the more skittish they both became, the more she was beginning to think a wedding was not a good idea. She became angry that she'd lost time, that she'd run out of time, that her choices were becoming increasingly limited. She had dated good men, bad men, the right men at the wrong time, the wrong men a lot of the time.

And the more time that passed, the more bitter he became, the more he wanted to go back in time, the more he craved his lost youth.

"Let's stay out," he'd say to friends after a party.

"Can't. We've got to get the sitter home."

"What's the point of having a baby-sitter if you're still completely tied down?"

"It's late," they'd say.

"It's early, it's very early," he'd say.

And soon there was nothing left to say.

"You're all so boring," he'd say, which didn't leave anyone feeling good about anything.

"Good night," they'd say.

He drove, the engine purred. They passed houses, lit for night, front porch lights on, upstairs bathroom light on, reading light on. He drove and she kept a lookout, fixed on the edges of the road, waiting to catch the eyes of an animal about to dash, the shadow of a deer about to jump.

When he got drunk, he'd start looking for a fight. If there wasn't another man around to wrestle with he'd turn on her.

"How can you talk incessantly all night and then the minute we're in the car you have nothing to say?"

"I had nothing to say all night either," she said.

"Such a fucking depressive—what's wrong with you?"

He accelerated.

"I'm not going to fight with you," she said.

"You're the kind of person who thinks she's always right," he said.

She didn't answer.

Coming into town the light was green. A narrow road, framed by hundred-year-old trees, a big white house on the left, an inn across the way, the pond where in winter ice-skaters turned pirouettes, the cemetery on the far side, the old windmill, the Episcopal church, all of it deeply picturesque.

Green light, go. Coming around the corner, he seemed to speed up rather than slow down, he seemed to press his foot harder into the gas. They turned the corner. She could tell they weren't going to make it. She looked at him to see if he had the wheel in hand, if he had any idea what he was doing, if he thought it was a joke. And then as they picked up more speed, as they slipped off the road, between two trees, over the embankment, she looked away.

The car stopped and her body continued on.

She remembers flying as if on a magic carpet, flying the way you might dream it, flying over water—sudden, surprising, and not entirely unpleasant.

She remembers thinking she might fly forever, all the way home.

She remembers thinking to cover her head, remembers they are by a cemetery.

She remembers telling herself—This is the last time.

She remembers when they went canoeing on the pond. A swan came charging toward the boat like a torpedo, like a hovercraft, skimming the surface, gaining on them. At first they thought it was funny and then it wasn't.

"Should I swing my paddle at him? Should I try and hit him on the head? Should I break his fucking neck? What should I do?" he kept asking, all the while leaving her at the front of the boat, paddling furiously, left, right, left, right.

Now, something is pecking at her, biting her.

There is a sharp smell like ammonia, like smelling salts.

She remembers her body not attached to anything.

"Can you hear us?"

"Can someone get the swans out of here?"

Splashing. People walking in water. A lot of commotion.

"Are you in pain?"

"Don't try to move. Don't move anything. Let us do all the work."

She remembers a lot of questions, time passing very slowly. She remembers the birds, a church, the leaf of a tree, the night sky, red lights, white lights in her eyes. She thinks she screamed. She meant to scream. She doesn't know if she can make any noise.

"What is your name?"

"Can you tell me your name?"

"Can you feel this?"

"We're going to give you some oxygen."

"We're going to set up an IV, there may be a little stick."

"Do these bites on your head hurt?"

"Follow this light with your eyes."

"Look at me. Can you look at me?"

He turns away. "We're going to need a medevac helicopter. We're going to need to land on that churchyard up there. We're going to need her stable, in a hard collar and on a board. I think we may have a broken neck."

She thinks they are talking about a swan, a swan has been injured.

"Don't go to sleep," they say, pinching her awake. "Stay with us."

And then she is flying again. She remembers nothing. She remembers only what they told her.

"You're very lucky. You could have been decapitated or paralyzed forever."

She is in a hospital far away.

"You have a facet dislocation, five over six—in essence, a broken neck. We're going to put you in a halo and a jacket. You'll be up and around in no time."

The doctor smiles down at her. "Do you understand what I'm saying?"

She can't nod. She tries to but nothing happens. "Yes," she says. "You think I'm very lucky."

In the operating room, the interns and residents swab four points on her head. "Have you ever done this before?" they ask each other.

"I've watched."

"We're going to logroll you," the doctor tells her. And

they do. "Get the raised part at the back of the skull and the front positioning pin lined up over the bridge of the nose, approximately seven centimeters over the eyebrows with equal distance between the head and the halo all the way around."

"How are your fingers? Can you move your fingers?"

She can.

"Good. Now wiggle your toes."

"You don't want it too high, it pitches the head back so she just sees sky, and you don't want it too low because then she's looking at her shoes," the doctor says. He seems to know what he is talking about.

"Feel my finger on your cheek—sharp or dull?"

"Sharp."

"Let's simultaneously tighten one anterior and its diagonal opposite posterior."

"Thanks. Now pass me the wrench."

"Close your eyes, please."

She doesn't know if they're talking to her or someone else. Someone looks directly down at her. "Time to close your eyes."

She is bolted into a metal halo, which is then bolted into a plastic vest, all of it like the scaffolding around a building, like the Statue of Liberty undergoing renovations. When they are done and sit her upright—she almost faints.

"Perfectly normal," the doctor says. "Fainting. Dizziness." He taps her vest—knock, knock.

"What am I made out of?"

"Space-age materials. In the old days we would have wrapped you in a plaster cast. Imagine how comfy that was. I assume you didn't have your seatbelt on?"

"Do these bites on your head hurt?" one of the residents asks.

"What bites?"

"Let's clean them, put some antibiotic on, and make sure she's up to date on tetanus," the doctor says. "Get some antibiotics on board just be to sure, you never know what was in that water."

"Where am I?"

"Stonybrook," the resident says as though that means something.

"Did someone say something about a swan?" she asks.

They don't answer.

Her grandmother is the first one who comes to see her. Ninety-seven years old, she gets her cleaning lady to drive her over.

"Your parents are in Italy, we haven't been able to reach them. The doctor says you're very lucky. You're neurologically intact."

"He was drunk."

"We'll sue the pants off them—don't worry."

"Did anything happen to him?"

"Broke a bone in his foot."

"I'm assuming he knows the wedding is off."

"If he doesn't, someone will tell him."

"Does that come off for bathing?" her grandmother points at the plastic vest.

"No. It's all bolted together."

"Well, that's what perfume was invented for."

Her girlfriends come in groups.

"We were fast asleep."

"We heard the sirens."

"I thought something exploded."

"He broke a bone in his foot?" she asks.

"His toe."

There is silence.

"You made the papers," someone says.

In the late afternoon, when she's alone, the innkeeper arrives.

"I saw it happen, I water the flowers at night right before bed. I was outside and saw your car at the light. Your fellow had the strangest expression on his face. The car surged forward, between the trees, it went out over the water and then nose-down into the muck. I saw you fly over the windshield, over the water. And he was standing up, pressed against the steering wheel, one hand in the air like he was riding a bucking bronco, his foot still on the gas, engine gunning, blowing bubbles into the water. I dialed 911. I went looking for you." He pauses. "I saw you flying through the air but I couldn't see where you landed."

A human gyroscope, a twirling top. She landed at her grandmother's house, a big old beach house on the block leading down to the ocean. She landed back in time, in the house of her youth. She sat on the porch, propped up in a wicker chair. Her grandmother read her stories of adventure and discovery. At night, when she was supposed to be sleeping, her mind wandered, daydreaming. She dreamt of a farmhouse by the water, of a small child hiding behind her skirt, a dog barking.

It was a summer in exile; off the party lists. No one knew which side to be on, there was talk of a lawsuit, "too ugly for summer," friends told her.

"To hell with them," her grandmother said. "I never liked any of them, their parents, or their grandparents. You're a young woman, you have your own life, what do you need to be married for? Enjoy your freedom. I never would have married if I could have gotten out of it." She leaned forward. "Don't tell anyone I told you that."

At ninety-seven her grandmother set her free.
At the end of the season her parents came home from Italy. "Pretend it never happened," her mother said. "Put yourself out there and in no time you'll meet someone new."

* * *

In the morning, she goes back to the beach, her hair smells of salt, her skin tastes of the sea, the scent of sex is on her, a sweet funk, a mixed drink, her and him and her, rising up, blending.

She goes back down to the beach, proud, walking like she's got a good little secret. As soon as she sees him, she blushes.

He doesn't know she is there, he doesn't know who she is, and what would he think if he knew?

She watches as he squirts white lotion from a tube, filling his hand with it, rubbing the hand over his chest, his belly, up and down his arms, over his neck and face, coating himself. He lubricates himself with lotion and then shimmies up the ladder and settles into the chair—on guard.

If he knew, would he think she was a crook, stealing him without his knowledge, or would he think it was nice to be desired, had from this strange distance?

Another boy, older, walks barefoot down the warm boards of the bathhouse, his feet moving fast and high, as if dancing on hot coals. She stays through the morning. He is not the only one, there are others. It is a constant low-key sex play, an ever-changing tableau.

This year they have new suits, their standard Speedos replaced with baggy red trunks. Beneath their trunks, they are naked, cocksure, tempting, threatening. It is always right there, the bulge, enjoying the rub of the fabric, the shrinking chill of the sea.

She watches how they work, how they sweep the deck of the bathhouse, set up umbrellas, how they respond to authority—taking direction from the man with the clipboard. Before settling on two or three of the strongest, most domi- nant, she watches how they play with each other. She chooses the one with the smoothest chest, and another with white hair, like feathers fanning out, crawling up his stom- ach, a fern bleached blond.

They are becoming themselves as she is losing herself.

* * *

It's not like she's been alone for the whole year—she's dated. I have a friend. We have a friend. He has a friend. The friend of a friend. He has four children from two marriages, they visit every other Saturday. He's a devoted father. I know someone else, a little afraid of commitment, good-looking, successful, never married. And then there's the widower—at least he understands grief.

The man from two marriages wants her to wear a strap-on dildo and whack him with a riding crop. The one afraid of commitment is impotent. Even that she doesn't mind until he tells her that it is because of her. The widower is sympathetic. He becomes determined to get her pregnant, "Don't worry," he says. "I'll put a bun in the oven." He comes before they even begin. "It's not for lack of trying," he says.

And then there's the one who never wants children. "I would never want to subject someone so innocent to the failings of my personality," he says. And she agrees.

The idea of them causes her gut to tighten.

The heat is gaining, the beach swelling with the ranks of the weekenders. It is Friday afternoon, they hit the sand acting as if they own it.

A whistle blows downwind, the boys grab the float and are into the water. "It's no game," the head honcho says as they pull someone out, sputtering.

Two cops in dark blue uniforms walk onto the beach and arrest a man lying on the sand. They take him away in handcuffs and flip-flops, his towel tossed over his shoulder. She overhears an explanation. "Violated an order of protection, stalking his ex-girlfriend. She saw him from the snack bar and dialed 911."

The temperature goes up.

She is sticky, salt-sticky, sex-sticky, too-much-sun-sticky. Walking back to the parking lot, she steps in something hot and brown. She walks on, hoping it's tar, knowing it's shit, walks rubbing her foot in the sand, wanting it off before she gets to the car.

The day is turning sour. In the drugstore, by the pharmacy counter, where a long line of people wait to pick up prescriptions for swimmer's ear, athlete's foot, Lyme disease, someone pinches her elbow.

She turns. Still sun-blind, she has the sensation of everything being down a dark tunnel, her eyes struggle to adjust.

"All better?" the woman asks.

She nods, still not sure whom she's talking to—someone from before.

"You don't come to the club anymore?"

She catches the woman looking into her basket: sunblock, bottled water, condoms, ovulation kits, plastic gloves, pregnancy tests, aspirin.

"Seeing somebody special?"

"Not really," she says.

"What's the saying—'Don't marry the ones you fuck? Don't fuck the ones you marry?' I can never remember how it goes."

She says nothing. She used to think she was on a par with the others, that for the most part she was ahead of the pack, and now it's as if she's fallen behind, out of the running. She feels the woman inspecting her, judging, looking through her basket, evaluating, as if about to issue her a summons, a reprimand for unconventional behavior.

At home, she showers, pours herself a glass of wine. If the accident threw her life off course, her grandmother's death made it clear that if this was something she wanted to do, she needed to do it soon, before it was too late. She pees on an ovulation stick, the stripe is positive—sometime within the next twenty-four hours the egg will be released. She pictures the egg in launch position, getting ready to burst out, she pictures it floating down her tubes, floating like slow-motion flying.

She slips back in time. A routine doctor's appointment, an annual occasion; naked in a paper robe, her feet in the stirrups.

"Come down a little closer," the doctor says. Using the speculum like pliers, he pries her open. He pulls the light closer and peers inside her.

"I've been wondering about timing—in terms of having a baby, how much longer do I have?"

"Have you ever been pregnant?"

"No," she says. "Never pregnant."

Everyone she knows has been pregnant, pregnant by boyfriends they hated, boyfriends who asked, Can't you get rid of it? or, worse yet, promised to marry them. Why has she never been pregnant? Was she too good, too boring, too responsible, or is there something else?

"Have you ever tried to get pregnant?"

"I haven't felt ready to start a family."

He continues to root around inside her. "You may feel a little scrape—that's the Pap test." She feels the scrape. "Try," he says. "That's the way to get pregnant, try and try again. It doesn't get any easier," he says, pulling the equipment out, snapping the gloves off.

Dressed, she sits in his office.

"I was thinking of freezing some eggs, saving them for later."

"If you want to have a baby, have a baby, don't freeze one." He scribbles something in her chart and closes it. He stands. "Give my regards to your mother. I never see her anymore."

"She had a hysterectomy ten years ago."

Sperm banks. She looked them up online; one sent a list of possible candidates categorized by ethnic background, age, height, and years of education, another sent a video with an infertile couple holding hands and talking about choosing donor insemination. She imagined what would happen later, when the child asked, Who is my father? She couldn't imagine saying R144, or telling the child that she'd chosen the father because he had neat handwriting, he liked the color green, and was "good with people." She would rather tell her child the story of the guards, and that she was born of the sea.

Her preparations begin in earnest at dusk. As other people are shaking up the martinis, she puts on her costume: her sex pants with nothing underneath, a silk undershirt, and then the insulated top she wore when they went skiing. She rubs Avon Skin So Soft over her hands, feet, face. She puts on two pairs of high socks, in part for warmth, in part to protect against sand fleas, ticks, mosquitoes. She pulls on a hooded sweat jacket, zips it, and looks in the mirror—perfectly unremarkable. She looks like one of those women who walk a dog alone at night, a mildly melancholy soul.

She fills the pockets of her sweat jacket with condoms—Friday night, there'll be lots of activity. She now thinks of herself as some sort of a sex expert, a not-for-profit hooker.

She cruises through town, stopping in at the local convenience store, ice cream parlor, pizza place, the parking lot behind the A&P, getting a feel for the night to come.

There are families walking down Main Street, fathers pushing strollers, mothers holding their toddlers' hands.

She hears the sound of a baby crying and has the urge to run toward it, believing that she alone understands the depth of that cry, profound, existential. There is something unnameable about her desire, unknowable unless you have found yourself looking at children wondering how you can wrest them from their parents, unknowable unless you have that same need. She wants to watch someone grow, unfold—she likes the name Mom.

She drives farther out of town, scouting. She goes to where they live—crash pads, shacks that would be uninhabitable if they weren't right by the beach. She knows where they live because one rainy afternoon she followed a truckload of them home.

There are no cars, no signs of life. A picnic table outside one of the shacks has a couple of half-empty glasses on it. The door is open—it's actually off its hinges, so she doesn't feel so bad going in.

Stepping inside, she breathes deeply, sharp perfume. Dark, dank, brown shag carpeting, a musty smell, like old sneakers—hard to know if it's the house or the boys. Bags of chips, Coke cans, dirty socks, T-shirts, pizza cartons on the counter. It's an overnight version of the guard shack. Four bedrooms, none of the sheets match. In the bathroom a large tube of toothpaste, a dripping faucet, grime, toilet seat up, a single bar of soap, two combs and a brush—all of it like a stable stall you'd want to muck out.

She pokes around, taking a T-shirt she knows belongs to her best boy. She takes a pair of shorts from another one, a baseball hat from a third, socks from a fourth. It's not that she needs so much, but this way no one will think much of it, at most it will be a load of laundry gone missing.

As though the boys were still at summer camp, their names are written into the back of their clothes, each in his own handwriting—Charlie, Todd, Travis, Cliff.

She drives back to town, to a different beach, moodier, more desolate. Hunkering down in the dunes, she immediately spots two people in the water—male and female. She takes out her birding glasses, identifying the boy—one of the older ones, diving naked into the waves. He swims toward the woman and she swims away. Hide and go seek. The woman comes out of the water, revealing herself, long brown hair, her body rounded and ripe, a woman, not a girl. He swims to shore, climbs out after her, and pulls her down onto the sand. She frees herself and runs back into the water. He goes after her and, pretending to rescue her, carries her out of the sea to a towel spread over the sand. They are like animals, tearing at each other. He stops for a moment, rummages through his clothing, takes something out—she can't see what, but she's hopeful. Their mating is violent, desperate. The woman both fights him and asks for more. He is biting the woman, mounting her from the back, the woman is on her hands and knees like a dog, and she seems to like it.

Finished, they pack up. They walk past her, see her, nod hello as though nothing ever happened. The woman is older, wild-looking, a kind of earthy goddess.

When they are gone she hurries across the sand. She finds the condom half covered in sand—limp debris. Something about the intensity of their coupling, so sexual, so graphic, leaves her not wanting to touch it. She unzips her fanny pack, pulls out a pair of latex examination gloves, pulls them on and then carefully rescues the sample—2.5 cc, usable if a little sandy.

She goes back to the car, assumes the position, and, making an effort to be discreet, inseminates. She stays in position for half an hour and then continues her rounds.

The romance of the hunt. She walks up and down looking for her men. The beaches are crowded with bonfires, picnics, catered parties. The air is filled with the scent of starter fluid, meat cooking; barbecue embers pulse, radiant red like molten lava.

She puts on the night-vision glasses, the world glows the green of things otherworldly and outside of nature. Everything is dramatic, everything is inverted, every gesture is evidence, every motion has meaning. She is seeing in the dark, seeing what can't be seen. A cigarette sails through the night like a tracer. She has to maximize, it's not enough to try just once, she wants to fill herself, she wants many, multiple, may the best man win. She wants competition, she wants there to be a race, a blend, she wants it to mix and match.

It is still early—the girl doesn't get off until ten or possibly eleven. She lies back in the sand, rubbing the points on her head where the screws were, dreaming. She glances up at the bathhouse. On the roof is a weather vane—a whale, a mounted Moby spinning north, south, east, west, to tell which way the wind blows, its outline sharp against the sky. She dreams of old whalers, fishermen, dreams she is in a boat, far from shore, in the middle of the open sea. She thinks of her grandmother, freeing her. She thinks of how proud her grandmother would be that she's taken things in hand.

Finally they arrive. Creatures of habit, they go back to the same spot where they were yesterday, this time moving with greater urgency. There is something genuine, heartfelt in the sex habits of the young—it is all new, thrilling, scary, a mutual adventure.

She retrieves and extracts her second sample. In the car, with her hips up high, she inseminates and she waits.

She imagines all of it mingling in her like sea foam. She imagines that with the sperm and the sand, she will make a baby born with pearl earrings in her ears.

In the local paper there is a notice for a childbirthing class. She goes, thinking she should be ready, she should know more. There are only two couples; a boy and girl still in high school and a local couple in their mid-thirties—the husband and wife both look pregnant, both sip enormous sodas throughout the class.

"When are you due?" the instructor asks each of them.

"In three weeks," the girl says, rubbing her belly, polishing the baby to perfection. "We didn't plan for the pregnancy, so we thought we better plan for the birth."

"Four weeks," the other woman says, sucking on her straw.

"And you?"

"I'm working on it," she says. And no one asks more.

On the table is an infant doll, a knitted uterus, and a bony pelvis.

"Your baby wants you," the childbirth teacher says, picking up the doll and passing it around.

The doll ends up with her. She holds it, thinking it would be rude to put it back down on the table—she might seem like a bad mother. She holds it, patting the plastic diaper of the plastic infant, pretending to comfort it. She sits the doll on her lap and continues taking notes: gestational age, baby at three weeks, three months, six months, nine months, dilation of the cervix, the stages of labor.

"All pregnancies end in birth," the instructor says, holding up the knitted uterus.

Leaving the hospital, she runs into the cop coming out of the emergency room.

"You all right?" she asks.

"Stepped on a rusty nail and had to get a tetanus shot." He rubs his arm. "So, how about that coffee?"

"Absolutely, before the end of summer," she says, getting into her car.

She is a woman waiting for her life to begin. She waits, counting the days. Her breasts are sore, full, like when they were first budding. She waits, thinking something is happening, and then it is not. There is a stain in her underwear, faint, light, like smoke, and overnight she begins to bleed. She bleeds thick, old blood, like rust. She bleeds bright red blood, like a gunshot wound. She bleeds heavily. She feels herself, hollow, fallow, failed. And bleeding, she mourns all that has not happened, all that will never happen. She mourns the boys, the men, the fiancé, her grandmother, the failings of her family, and her own peculiar shortcomings that have put her in this position.

She becomes all the more determined to try again. She counts the days, keeps her temperature charts and watches her men.

She will try harder, making sure that on the two most viable days she gets at least two doses—no such thing as too much. She continues to prepare. August, high tide, peak of the season. The local newspapers are thick with record numbers of deer jumping in front of cars, a drowning on an unprotected beach, shark spottings. The back pages are filled with pictures of social events: the annual hospital gala, the museum gala, the celebrity tennis match, benefit polo, golf tournaments, the horse show. This summer's scandal involves a man who tried to get into "the" country club, was loudly rejected, and then showed up at the front door every day waiting for someone to sign him in as their guest.

She makes a coffee date with the cop. At the last minute he calls to cancel.

"They've got me on overtime. Can I get a rain check?"

"Yes," she says, "but it's not raining."

She goes on with her rounds, her anthropological education. She gets bolder. Out of curiosity she goes to the other beach, the one she has always heard about, notorious for late-night activity.

There are men in the dunes, men who tell their wives that they're running out for milk, or a pack of cigarettes, and find themselves prowling, looking for relief. With her night-vision glasses she can see it all quite clearly; rough, animalistic, horrifying and erotic—pure pornography.

A Planned Parenthood vigilante, throughout her cycle, she continues distributing the condom supply. She wants to keep them in the habit; she wants them to practice safe sex. She tracks her boys; she has to keep up, to know their rhythms and routines. She has to know where to find them when the moment is right. She adds a new one to her list, a sleeper who's come into his own over the course of the summer—Travis. An exceptional swimmer, it is Travis who goes into the undertow like a fish. He puts his fins on, walks backward into the water and takes off.

Every morning he is in the water, swimming miles of laps back and forth, up and down—the ocean is his Olympic-sized pool. Sometimes she swims with him. She puts herself in the water where he is; she feels her body gliding near his. She swims a quarter mile, a half mile, moving with the current. She feels the sting of the salt in her eyes, strings of seaweed like fringe hanging off her ankles, the tug of the riptide. She swims not thinking she could be carried out to sea but that she is a mermaid and this is her habitat. She swims to the next lifeguard stand, gets out, and walks back, having perfected walking on sand, keeping her feet light, barely making a mark.

It is nearly the end of summer. She has been taking her temperature, peeing on sticks, waiting for the surge that tells her she's ripe, ready.

Late afternoon at Main Beach, her boys assemble to be photographed for the town Christmas card. They pile onto the stand, wearing red Santa hats, sucking in their stomachs, flexing their muscles. On cue they smile. She stands behind the official photographer and, with her own camera, clicks.

Does it matter to her which of them is the father of her child, whose sperm succeeds? She likes the unknowing, the possibility that it could be any one of a number of them, and then sometimes she thinks she wants it to be him, the boy with the hieroglyph, with the baby-sitter/waitress girlfriend—he strikes her as the most stable, most sincere.

Soon they will go back to school and the summer romance will end. They will leave and she will stay on.

The day the stick turns positive, she makes her rounds.

Travis has a new girlfriend, a blonde who works at the snack bar. She finds them on the other side of town by the marina. They make out for more than forty minutes before Travis leads her to a platform at the end of the dock. When they are done, they dive into the water for a quick swim and she finds herself checking her watch, worrying that the sperm is getting cold. When they leave she has trouble locating the condom, finally finding it, dangling from a nail on one of the pilings almost as though he knew and left it for her. Five cc—a very good shot.

She inseminates herself, lying back in the car, knees hooked over the steering wheel, blanket over her for warmth. It is cooler in the evenings now; she has a layer of long underwear on under her sex outfit, and a spare blanket in the car. The boys and girls all wear sweatshirts declaring their intentions, preferences, fantasies: Dartmouth, Tufts, SUNY, Princeton, Hobart, Columbia, NYU.

She lies back, looking up at the sky; there is a full moon, a thousand stars, Orion, Taurus, the Big Dipper. She lies waiting and then moves on. The wind is starting to blow. At the end of every summer there is always a storm, a violent closing out of the season, it charges through literally changing the air—the day it passes, fall begins.

Her favorite couple is hidden in a curve of dune. They are already at it when she arrives. Leaving the night-vision glasses in the car, she travels by moonlight with just her fanny pack. The wind is hurling sand across the dune; the surf crashes unrelentingly. They do it fast, now practiced, they do it seriously, knowing this will be one of the last times, they do it and then they run for cover.

The condom is still warm when she finds it. She holds it between her teeth and, using both hands, scoops the sand, molding it into a mound that will hold her hips up high. She inseminates herself lying in the spot where they had lain. She inseminates, listening to the pounding of the waves, the sea ahead of the storm, watching moonlight shimmering across the water.

A phosphorescent dream: she thinks she feels it, she

thinks she knows the exact moment it happens; the sperm and the egg finding each other, penetrating, exploding, dividing, floating, implanting, multiplying. She imagines a sea horse, a small, curled thing, primitive, growing, buds of hands—fists clenched, a translucent head, eyes bulging. She feels it digging in, feeding, becoming human. She wakes up hungry, ready. In May she will meet her, a little girl, just in time for summer—Georgica.

REMEDY

It is about wanting and need, wanting and need—a peculiar, desperate kind of need, needing to get what you never got, wanting it still, wanting it all the more, nonetheless. It is about a profound desire for connection. It is about how much we don't know, how much we can't say, what we don't understand. It is about how unfamiliar even the familiar can become.

It is about holding one's breath, holding the breath until you are blue in the face, holding the breath to threaten, to dare, to say if you do not give me what I want, I will stop breathing. It is about holding back, withholding. It is about being stuck. It is about panic. It is about realizing you are in over your head, something's got to give. It is about things falling apart. It is about fracture.

It is afternoon, just after lunch. She starts dialing. She dials, knowing no one is home. Her mother, retired, remains a worker, always out, doing, running. Her father is busy as well, taking classes, volunteering. She dials as a kind of nervous tic and then, when she can't get the call to go through, she dials more frantically as though in a nightmare; calling for help, screaming and no one hears, picking up to find the line is dead. She dials, forgetting the new area code.

"The area code for the number you're calling has

changed. The new area code is 343. Please redial the number using the new area code."

She dials again, unsure of the last four digits of her calling card.

"The personal identification number you entered is incorrect. Please reenter the last four digits of your calling card."

She reenters.

"I'm sorry."

She is cut off.

She dials once more—if it doesn't work, she is going to dial 0 and have an operator place the call, she is going to dial 911 and tell them it is an emergency, somebody must do something. She dials 9 for an outside line and then she dials the number straight through, letting the office pay for the call—fuck it. The new area code feels odd on her fingers. She hates change, she absolutely hates change.

And then the phone is ringing, and on the second ring the answering machine picks up, and there is her mother's voice, distant, formal—the outgoing announcement of a generation that has never gotten used to the answering machine.

She hangs up without leaving a message.

She checks her schedule. There is a three o'clock meeting—the subject: pain relief.

She has not spoken to Steve today. That part of their relationship, calls during the day, is over. There used to be phone calls as soon as he walked out of the apartment, sometimes from the elevator going down, "I'm in the elevator, the neighbors are surrounding me, pick up the phone." A call when he got to the office, "Just checking in," after lunch, "I shouldn't have had the wine," in the late afternoon, "I'll be finished early," and then again before leaving, "What do you want to do about dinner?"

Now, they can't talk. Every conversation, every attempt turns into a fight. She can't say the right thing, he can't do the right thing, they hate each other—all the more for the disappointment. There is no negotiation, no interest in repair, only anger and inertia.

"It's not my fault," he says.

"If there's such a thing as fault—it's half your fault."

She hurries to prepare for the meeting, the launch of a combination acetaminophen/homeopathic preparation (Tylenol and Rescue Remedy)—Products for Modern Living, a pill for all your problems.

Wendy, the shared assistant, stops her as she's going down the hall. "I couldn't get you a conference room for a whole hour, so I got you two halves."

"Two halves of a conference room?"

"From three to three-thirty you're in two, and from three-thirty until four you're in six."

"Halfway through, we have to change rooms? That's crazy."

Wendy shrugs.

"It's not just about any headache," she says, sitting down with the client. "It's your headache. It's the sense that you're about to explode. Your head is pounding, the boss is droning on in the background, kids are screaming, you need relief and you need it fast."

The client nods.

"It's the classic headache ad—pumped up, there's throbbing and there's volume and pressure."

"Modern life is very stressful," the client says, happily counting the bucks.

"There's the emergency room doctor/trauma surgeon, the voice of authority. 'As a doctor at a leading trauma hospital, I know about pain, I know about stress, and I know how quickly I need to feel better.' The doctor moves through the emergency room—all kinds of horrible things are happening in the background. 'A combination of acetaminophen and a homeopathic supplement, Products for Modern Living offers safe, effective relief.' She picks up a patient's chart and makes a note. 'Sometimes what's old is what's new.'"

"I like it. It's fresh and familiar," the client says.

"Let's move from here into conference room six and we'll review the rest of our campaign," she says, seamlessly moving her team down the hall.

Later, she passes Wendy's desk; Wendy is obsessively dipping cookies into a container of orange juice.

"Are you okay?"

Wendy puts out her hands, they're shaking. "Low blood sugar. I spent from eight-thirty until three trying to get the damned computer to print. I called Information Services, they said they could come tomorrow, but the proposal had to go out today. Never mind. I did it. I got it done." She plunges a cookie into the juice.

She hands Wendy a sample of the remedy. "Try it," she says. "Call it market research and bill them for an extra twenty-five hundred bucks."

Again she dials. The phone rings and rings, maybe her mother is there, maybe she is on the other line. Maybe it is her father—her father always ignores the call-waiting, he doesn't know what call-waiting is.

"Didn't you hear me beeping? That was me trying to call you."

"Is that what that was? I was on the line, talking to a man about something."

She worries that one day she will call and no one will answer—one day she will call and they won't be there anymore.

She remembers dialing her grandmother's number just after her grandmother died. She called just as she had always done. The number rang and rang and somehow she didn't lose hope that her grandmother would find her way to the phone. She thought it might take longer, but she expected her grandmother would answer. And then one day there was a recorded voice, "The number you are trying to reach has been disconnected. If you need further assistance please hang up and dial the operator."

She hangs up. Six months after her grandmother died, she went to her grandmother's house and parked outside the front door. The plants that used to be on the sill of the kitchen window were gone. The light in the living room, always on, was off. She walked around back and peered through the sliding glass door. The house was filled with different furniture; different pictures of different grandchildren rested on the mantel.

"Can I help you?" Mr. Silver, the old man next door asked, as though he'd never seen her before.

"Just looking," she said and walked away.

It is getting dark: five-twenty-two. If she hurried she could take the six o'clock Metroliner, she could be in Washington by eight. She wants to go home. It has been coming upon her for days. Almost like coming down with a cold, she has been coming down with the urgent need to go home, to sit at her place at the kitchen table, to look out her bedroom window at the trees she saw at one, at twelve, at twenty. She needs something, she can't say exactly what. She keeps brushing it off, hoping it will pass, and then it overwhelms her.

Again, she dials. A man answers. She hangs up and tries again, more carefully, looking at the numbers. Again, the unfamiliar man answers.

"Sorry," she says. "Wrong number."

Again, she tries again.

"May I help you?" he says.

"I keep thinking I'm calling home, I know this number, and yet you answer. Sorry. I'll check the number and try again."

She dials.

"Hello?" the man says. "Hello, hello?"

She says nothing.

He waits and then hangs up.

She puts on her coat and leaves the office. If she had reached her mother she might have felt good enough to go to the gym or to go shopping. But what started as a nervous tic has become something more, she is all the more uncomfortable, she goes directly to the apartment.

There is a message from Steve.

"Sorry we didn't talk. I meant to call earlier but things got crazy. Tonight's the game. I'll be home late."

The game. She forgot.

She takes off her coat and pours herself a glass of wine.

Steve is at the game with his best friend, Bill. Bill is forty-three, never married. Bill won't keep anything perishable in his apartment and has no plants because it's too much responsibility. When he's bored he drones "Next," demanding a change of subject. Inexplicably, it is Bill whom Steve turns to for advice.

Again, she dials.

"Who are you trying to reach?" the man asks. This time, no hello.

Without saying anything, she hangs up.

She orders Chinese. She calls her brother in California; she gets his machine. "When did you last talk to Mom and Dad? Were they okay? Did something happen to their phone? Call me."

By ten, she is beginning to imagine horrible things, accidents. She is dialing and dialing. Where are they? At seventy-six and eighty-three, how far can they have gotten?

She remembers New Year's Eves when she was young, when she was home eating Ruffles with Ridges and California Dip, watching New Year's Rockin' Eve and waiting.

Eleven-fifty-nine, the countdown, sixty seconds away from a new year; three, two, one. The ball drops. The crowd goes crazy.

"Happy New Year from Times Square in New York. Look and listen as America welcomes in 1973." She drinks her fizzy cider and waits. Ten minutes later the phone rings.

"Happy New Year, sweetie," her mother says. "We're having a wonderful time. Mrs. Griswald is just about to serve dessert and then we'll be home. It's going to be a good year."

She remembers checking the clock—twelve-twenty. At one, New Year's Rockin' Eve segued into the late, late movie and she began to wonder. At one-thirty wonder turned to worry. At quarter of two she was picturing her parents' car in a ditch by the side of the road. At two-twenty she wondered if it was too late to call the Griswalds and ask when they'd left. She was twelve years old and powerless. By two-forty, when she heard their key in the door, she was livid. She slammed the door to her room and turned off the light.

"Honey, are you all right?"

"Leave me alone."

"I hope she didn't get into the liquor—should I check?"

"I hate you."

Happy New Year.

She gives it one last go—if they don't answer, she is going to call Mrs. Lasky, one of the neighbors, and ask if things are as odd as they seem.

Her mother answers on the first ring.

"Where were you?" she blurts.

"I was in the closet, looking for something."

"I've been trying to call you for hours, why do you sound so strange?"

"Strange?"

"Breathless."

"I was in the closet—foraging. What do you mean you've been calling for hours, we just got home. We had concert tickets."

"I didn't know where you were. I was worried."

"We're adults, Susan. We're allowed to go out." She pauses. "What day is it?"

"Wednesday."

"You usually call on Sunday."

"I was thinking of coming home."

"When?"

"This weekend."

"Well, I don't know what our schedule is like. I'll have to check. What's new?" her mother asks, changing the subject.

"Not much. I must have dialed your number a hundred times—first I couldn't get through, then I got the machine, and the last few times some man answered. I was beginning to feel like I was losing my mind."

"That must have been Ray."

"Ray?"

"A friend of your father's."

"Daddy doesn't have any friends."

"This is someone he met at one of his classes—I think he's lonely, he brought his cat. It's good you're not here." She is allergic to cats.

"I thought it was me, I thought I dialed wrong. Why didn't he identify himself? Why didn't he say, Green residence? Why didn't he just say—I'm the one who's out of place?"

"I don't know," her mother says.

"Did Daddy go with you to the concert?"

"Of course—he drove."

"What was this Ray doing at the house when you weren't home?"

"Haven't I mentioned him?"

"No."

"Really? You would think I would have—he's staying with us."

There is a long pause.

"Mother—could you just check with your doctor, could

you just say, my daughter is concerned. She thinks I don't remember. She thinks I forget. Could you do me the favor and ask the doctor if everything is all right?"

"The truth is when I'm in there, I don't think of it."

"You forget."

"I'm in that paper gown. Who can think of anything when you feel like at any second it might come undone?"

"How long has this Ray been around?

"A couple of weeks. He's a lovely guy. You'd like him. He's very tidy."

"Is he paying rent?"

"No," her mother says, horrified. "He's a friend of your father's." She changes the subject. "Where's Steve?"

"At the game." As she says it, she hears Steve at the door. She hurries to get off the phone. "I'll call you tomorrow, we'll figure out the weekend." She snaps the bedroom light off.

She hears Steve in the living room, opening the mail. She hears him in the kitchen, opening the fridge. She sees his shadow pass down the hall. He is in the bathroom, peeing, then brushing his teeth. He comes into the bedroom, half undressed. "It's only me," Steve says. "Don't get excited."

She doesn't respond.

"Are you in here?" He turns on the light.

"I just spoke to my mother."

"Yeah? It's Wednesday—don't you normally talk to them on Sunday?"

"There is a strange man living at the house. He's been there for two weeks—she forgot to tell me. A friend of my father's."

"Your father doesn't have any friends."

"Exactly."

"Maybe if you'd waited and called on Sunday, he wouldn't have been there." Steve pulls his T-shirt off and drops it onto the floor.

"Not funny." She gestures toward the hamper. "I was thinking I should go and see my parents this weekend—that's why I was calling. I haven't been in a long time. But I can't exactly go home if this guy is there."

"Stay in a hotel."

She sits up to set the alarm. "I'm not staying in a hotel. Am I going to have to do some sort of intervention, kidnap my parents and reprogram them?"

"It's deprogram."

"How's Bill?"

"Good."

"Did you ask him what you should do?"

"About what?" Steve punches at his pillow.

"Us."

Steve doesn't answer. She thinks of her parents, her parents' marriage. She thinks of her parents, of Steve, of having children, of when they stopped talking about it. She wishes they had children. He thinks it's good they didn't. She still wants to have one. "It's not going to fix it," he says. She doesn't want the child to fix it. She wants the child because she wants a child and she knows that without Steve she will not have children. She rolls away from him. There is an absence of feeling, a deadness, an opaque zone where there used to be more.

"Breathe," Steve says to her.

"What?"

"You weren't breathing. You were doing that holding-your-breath thing."

She takes a deep breath. Sighs.

"Do you want me to come with you to your parents?"

"No."

In the night, in the subtlety of sleep, they are drawn together, but when they wake it is as though they remember—they pull apart, they wake up en garde.

"I know it's been hard," he says in the morning as they're getting ready to go.

"What should we do?" she asks.

"I don't know," he says.

They don't say anything more. She is afraid to talk, afraid of what is happening, afraid of what she is feeling, afraid of what will happen next, afraid of just about everything.

The morning meeting is adult undergarments—Peer Pampers. There are boxes of the product on the conference room table. The client opens a box and starts passing them around—a cross between maxi-pads and diapers, there's something about them that's obscene.

"What we're selling here is a new gel insert—it's incredibly absorbent," the client says. He is the only one truly comfortable handling the product—he rips one of the diapers open, pulls apart the crotch area to expose the insert. "This is it," he says. "It sucks up water, up to ten ounces. Our research shows the average void is four to eight. The older you get, the more frequently you urinate and with slightly less volume, so we're estimating approximately six to seven ounces per use."

A junior creative executive picks up one of the garments and, as though giving a demonstration, pours his coffee in. "Afraid to have your morning cup because it runs right through you? Try these."

For a tenth of a second it's funny and then, as a liquidy brown stain spreads through the material, it becomes a problem. Blushing, he puts the dirty diaper in the trash.

"Not a good idea," someone says. "A very poopy diaper."

"That's all right," the client says. "Accidents happen."

"It's a control issue," she says, trying to pull the meeting back to order. "How to feel in control when you are out of control. Picture a man in his car stuck in traffic, a woman strapped into her seat on an airplane, she coughs. But she doesn't look stressed; in fact she's smiling. When everything around you feels out of control, help yourself feel in control. One less worry."

"Don't make it seem like we're encouraging people to piss their pants," the client says.

"The idea is to encourage people to lead healthy, normal

lives, not to let bladder control issues stop them from activities that are part of everyday life. We'll spend some time with these," she says, gathering up the diapers. "Give us a call next week."

The client stands. There's a wet spot on his suit.

"I know what you're thinking," he says, "but it's not that. In the car on the way here—my muffin flipped. I got jam all over me. Imagine me," he says, "going through the day with a wet spot on my suit selling adult diapers."

"There's a one-hour cleaner down the block, maybe they can do something for you," she says.

"Now that's a good idea."

Steve calls. "I was wondering if we could have dinner?"

She thinks two thoughts—he wants them to work it out and he's leaving. Either way, whatever it is, she doesn't want to hear it. She isn't ready.

"I have plans," she says.

"Yeah, what?"

"I'm meeting Mindy for a drink. She's coming in for a matinee and then I'm meeting her."

"Well, I'll see you later then. What should I do about dinner?"

"Don't wait for me," she says.

She has no plans. She hasn't talked to Mindy in six months.

"Are you okay?" Steve asks.

"Fine," she says. "You?"

"Fine," he says. "Fucking fantastic."

After work she goes to Bloomingdale's. She wanders for two hours. She is tempted to take herself to a movie, to take herself to a bar and have a drink, to get home really late, really drunk, but she doesn't have the energy.

"Are you finding everything you need?" an overzealous sales associate wants to know.

What does she want? What does she need? She is thinking about Steve, trying to imagine a life apart. She's afraid that if they separate she will evaporate, she will cease to exist. He'll be fine, he'll hardly notice that she is gone. She hates him for that. Will she start dating? She can't picture it, can't imagine starting again with someone else.

When she gets home, Steve is on the bed, channel surfing. "I ate the Chinese—I hope you weren't saving it."

"I ate with Mindy," she says.

She goes into the kitchen. Dials.

Ray answers.

"Hello, is Mrs. Green there?"

"May I ask who's calling?"

She wants to say—you know damn well who's calling, but instead she pauses and then says, "Her daughter."

"One moment." There is a long pause and then Ray returns. "She's not available right now, may I take a message?"

"Yes, could you ask her to call me as soon as she is available. Thank you." She hangs up.

"Find anything?" Steve calls from the bedroom.

She doesn't respond. She stands in front of the open fridge, grazing.

The phone rings. "It's deeply disturbing to call home and have to ask to speak with your parents. What does that mean, you're not available?" she says.

"I was in the bathroom. I fell asleep in the tub."

"Why didn't he just say that?"

"He was being discreet."

"You're my mother. Does he know that?"

"Of course he knows."

"Why was he answering the phone? Why didn't Dad get it?"

"Maybe Dad was busy, maybe Dad didn't hear it, he doesn't hear as well as he used to. We're old, you know."

"You're not old. Who is this Ray character anyway? How much do you know about him?"

Her mother doesn't say anything.

"Mom, are you there? Is he right there? Can you not talk because the guy, the guest, the visitor, Ray, is right there?"

"Yes. Of course."

"Yes, of course, he's there? Can he hear you? Can you not talk because he can hear you?"

"No, not at all."

She stops for a minute, she takes a breath. "I feel like the SWAT team should be setting up next door with sharpshooters and a hostage negotiator. Are you all right? Are you safe?"

She overhears a mumbled conversation: "Oh thank you. Just milk, no sugar, thanks Ray." There is a slurping sound.

"Where does this Ray sleep?"

"Downstairs, in your brother's room. What train are you planning on taking?"

"I think I can get out early, two o'clock."

"We'll look forward to seeing you. Stay in touch."

She hangs up.

"When are you leaving?" Steve asks.

"Early afternoon—I'll go straight from the office."

"Should we talk?" he says.

"Are you seeing somebody?"

"No. Are you?"

"No. Then we don't have to talk."

She walks into the bedroom. "This is how we're having a conversation, yelling back and forth between rooms?"

"Apparently."

"Is this how Bill told you to do it?"

He doesn't say anything.

"There's some man living in my parents' house. Can't the rest of it wait?"

"Do you want to have a code word so you can tell me if something is really wrong?"

"I'll say, it's unbelievably hot. And that means call the police or something."

"Unbelievably hot," Steve says.

"And if I say my toes are cold, that means I'm confused and you should ask me some more questions."

"Hot house/cold toes, got it."

In the morning, Wendy's desk is too neat.

"Did she quit?" asks Tom, the executive who shares Wendy with Susan.

"She just needed a day off; the computer got to her."

By nine there's a temp in Wendy's place, a woman who arrives with her own name plate—MEMORABLE TEMPORARIES, MY NAME IS JUDY.

"Worst thing is not knowing someone's name, looking at her and wondering, Who is she? How can I ask her to do anything—I don't know her name. Now you know, it's Judy. And I'm here to help you."

"Thank you, Judy" she says, going into her office and closing the door.

"I have an appointment outside—I won't be back," she tells Judy at one-fifteen, when she emerges, wheeling her suitcase down the hall.

"Have a good weekend," Judy says with a wink.

The train pulls out—she has the sense of having left something behind, something smoldering, something worrisome—Steve.

The train pushes through the tunnel, rocking and rolling. It pops out over the swamps of New Jersey, and suddenly instead of skyscrapers and traffic there are swamps, leggy white egrets, big skies, chemical plants, abandoned factories, and the melancholy beauty of the afternoon light.

She takes a taxi from the train. Directing the driver toward home, she descends into a world that is half memory, half fantasy, a world so fundamentally at her core that it is hard to know what is real, what is not, what was then, what is now.

"Is there somebody home?" the driver asks, pulling up to the dark house.

"There's a key under the pot," she says, giving away the family secret.

It is twilight. She stands in the driveway, with her suitcase at her feet, watching light fade from the sky, wondering why she came home. On the telephone line above her, four crows sit waiting. The trees press in like dark shields, she listens to the breeze, to the birds still calling. Across the way she sees Mrs. Altman moving around in her kitchen. In the house that used to belong to the Walds, someone new is also doing the dinner dance.

She stands watching the sky, the branches of trees blackening against the dusk. There is a rustling in the woods beyond the house. She glances at the brush, expecting to see a dog or a child taking a shortcut home.

Her father pushes out, breaking twigs along the way. He is carrying a brown paper bag and a big stick.

"Dad?"

"Yeah?"

"Are you okay?"

"Yeah, I'm fine. I walked."

"Did you have car trouble?"

"Oh no," he says. "I didn't have any trouble. I took the scenic route." Her father peers into the carport. "Ray's not here? I must have beat him."

"Where's your car?"

"I left it with Ray. He had errands to run. I had a very nice walk. I went through the woods."

"You're eighty-three years old, you can't just go through the woods because it's more scenic."

"What would anyone want with me? I'm an old man."

"What if you fell or twisted your ankle?"

He waves his hand, dismissing her. "I could just as easily fall here at home and no one would notice." He bends to get the key. "You been here long?"

"Just a few minutes."

Her father opens the door, she steps inside, expecting the dog. She has forgotten that the dog is not there anymore, he died about a year ago.

"That's so strange—I was expecting the dog."

"Oh," her father says. "I do that all the time. I'm always thinking I shouldn't leave the door open, shouldn't let the dog out. We have him, for you, if you want," her father says. "His ashes are on the shelf over the washing machine. Do you want to take him with you?"

"If we could leave him for now, that would be good," she says.

"It's your dog," her father says. "So, how long are you here for?"

"I don't know."

"You don't usually stay long."

She takes her bag down the hall to her room. The house is still. It is orderly and neat. Everything is exactly the same and yet different. The house is smaller, her room is smaller, the twin bed is smaller. There is a moment of panic—a fear of being consumed by whatever it is that she came in search of. She feels worse, further from herself. She looks around, wondering what she is doing in this place, it is deeply familiar and yet she feels entirely out of place, out of sorts. She wants to run, to take the next train back. From her bedroom window she sees her mother's car glide into the driveway.

"Is she here?" She hears her mother's voice across the house.

"Hi Mom," she says and her mother does not hear her. She tries again. "Hi Mom." She walks down the hall saying, Hi Mom, Hi Mom, Hi Mom at different volumes, in different intonations, like a hearing test.

"Is that you?" her mother finally asks when she's two feet away.

"I'm home."

Her mother hugs her—her mother is smaller too. Everything is shrinking, compacting, intensifying. "Did you have a
good flight?"

She has never flown home. "I took the train."

"Is Ray back?" her mother asks.

"Not yet," her father says as he puts two heaping table-
spoons of green powder into a glass of water.

"Where did you meet this Ray?"

"Your father left his coat at the health food store and Ray
found it and called him."

Her father nods. "I went to get the coat and we started
talking."

"Your father and Ray go to vitamin class together."

"Vitamin class?"

"They go to the health store and a man speaks to them
over a video screen."

"What does the man tell you?"

"He talks about nutrition and health. He tells us what to
do."

"How many people go?"

"About thirty." Her father stirs, tapping the side of the
glass with his spoon. "This is the green stuff, I have two
glasses of this twice a day and then I have a couple of the red
stuff. It's all natural." He drinks in big gulps.

It looks like a liquefied lawn.

"See my ankles," he says, pulling up the leg of his pants.
"They're not swollen. Ever since I started taking the supplements, the swelling has gone down. I feel great. I joined a
gym."

"Where was this Ray before he came to you?"

"He had a place over on Arlington Road, one of those
apartments behind the A&P, with another fellow."

"Something happened to that man, he may have died or
gone into a home. I don't really know," her mother says.

There is the sound of a key in the door.

"That's Ray."

The door opens. Ray comes in carrying groceries.

"In your honor, Ray is making vegetable chow mein for dinner," her mother says. And she is not sure why vegetable chow mein is in her honor.

"You must be Ray," she says, putting her hand out as Ray puts the bags down.

"You must be the daughter," Ray says, ignoring her hand.

"Did you get the crispy noodles?" her mother asks.

"I don't eat meat anymore," her father says. "I don't really eat much of anything. At my age, I don't have a big appetite."

"I got you some chocolate rice milk—I think you'll like it." Ray hands her father a box of milk.

"I like chocolate," her father says.

"I know you do." Ray is of indeterminate age, somewhere between fifty-five and sixty-five, sinewy with close-cropped hair, like a skullcap sprinkled with gray. Each of his features belongs to another place; he is a little bit Asian, a little bit Middle Eastern, a little bit Irish, and within all that he is incredibly plain and without affect, as though he has spent a lot of time trying not to be.

"And I got the noodles," Ray says.

"Oh good," her mother says. "I like things that are crunchy."

Her mother and father peer into the grocery bags. She wonders if Ray pays for these groceries—if that's why they're so interested—or if he makes them pay for it.

"Nuts," her father says, pulling out a bag of cashews. "And raisins."

"Organic," Ray says, winking.

Her father loves anything organic.

"Remember when we couldn't have lettuce because it wasn't picked by the right people, and then we couldn't have grapes. And after that it was something else," she says.

"Tuna," her mother says, "because of the dolphins."

"I have something to show you," her father says, leading

Ray into the living room. There is a drawing on the dining table.

"Very nice," Ray says.

Her mother walks past them. She sits at the piano and begins to play. "I've started my lessons again."

"Let's hear the Schubert," Ray says.

Her father proudly shows her more drawings. "I'm taking classes, at the college. Free for seniors."

It is incredibly civilized and all she can think about is how bad things are with Steve and that she needs to come up with a slogan for adult diapers by Monday.

A little later, she is sitting in the den. As her mother knits, they watch the evening news. Her father is in the bedroom, blasting the radio. Ray is in the kitchen with the pots and pans. The smell of garlic and scallions fills the house.

"You let him just be in the kitchen? You don't worry what he does to the food—what he puts in it?"

"What's he going to do—poison us?" her mother says. "I'm tired of cooking. If I never cook again that's fine with me."

She looks at her mother—her mother is a good cook, she is what you'd call a food person.

"Does Ray have a crush on Dad?"

"Don't be ridiculous—what am I, chopped liver?" Her mother inhales. "Smells good doesn't it?"

A noise, an occasional small sound draws her out of the room and down the hall. She moves quietly thinking she will catch him, she will catch Ray doing something he shouldn't.

She finds him on the living room floor, sitting on a cushion. There are small shiny cymbals on his first and third fingers and every now and then he pinches his fingers together—*ping*.

She goes back into the den.

"He's meditating," her mother says, before she even asks. "Twice a day for forty minutes. He tried to get your father to do it and me too. We don't have the patience. Sometimes we sit with him, we cheat, I read, your father falls asleep."

Again there is the sound of the cymbals—*ping*.

"Isn't that the nicest sound?"

"Does he do it at specific intervals?"

"He does it whenever his mind begins to wander. He goes very deep. He's been at it for twenty years."

"Where is Ray from? Does he have a family? Does he have a job? Is he part of a cult?"

"Why are you so suspicious? Did you come all the way home to visit or to investigate us?"

"I came home to talk to you."

"I don't know that I have anything to say," her mother says.

"I need advice—I need you to tell me what to do."

"I can't. It's your life. You do what's right for you." She pauses. "You said you wanted to come home because you needed to get something, you wanted something—what was it, something you left in your room?"

"I don't know how to describe it," she catches herself. "It's something I never got. Something from you," she says.

"I don't really have much to give. Call some friends, make plans, live it up. Aren't any of your high school buddies around?"

She is thirty-five and suddenly needs her mother. She is thirty-five and doesn't remember who her high school buddies were.

"What does Ray want from you? What does he get?"

"I have no idea. He doesn't ask for anything. Maybe just being here is enough, maybe that's all he wants. Everyone doesn't need as much as you."

There is silence.

"Damn," her mother says. "I dropped a stitch."

She leaves the room. She goes downstairs. She wants to see exactly what he is up to.

The door to her brother's room is cracked open. She pushes it further. A brown cat is curled up on a pillow; it looks at her. She steps inside. The cat dives under the bed.

The room is clean and neat. Everything is put away. There

is no sign of life, except for the dent in the pillow where the cat was, and a thin sweater folded over the back of a chair. By the side of the bed is a book of stories, an empty water glass, and an old alarm clock, ticking loudly.

"Can I help you?"

Ray is in the room. She doesn't know how he got there, how he got down the stairs without a sound.

"I was just looking for a book," she says.

"What book?"

She blushes as though this were a quiz. "Robinson Crusoe." She knows it is a book her brother had, a book they used to look at as children.

He takes the book from the shelf and hands it to her.

She sneezes. "Cat," she says.

"Bless you," he says. "You'll excuse me," he says, edging her out of the room. "I want to refresh myself before dinner."

In the downstairs bathroom, each of his personal effects is arranged in a tight row on top of a folded towel—toothbrush, comb, nail clippers.

The cat's litter box is in the corner. There are four little lumps in it, shit rolled in litter, dirt balls dusted in ash.

Her mother sits at the table. "I haven't had chow mein since Aunt Lena used to make it with leftover soup chicken."

There is the scrape of a matchstick. Ray lights two tall tapers.

"Every night we have candles," her father says. "Ray makes the effort."

Ray has changed his clothes, he's wearing an orange silk shirt, he seems to radiate light. "From the Goodwill," he says, seeming to know what she is thinking. "It must have been a costume. In the back of the neck, in black marker, it's written—'Lear.'"

"I'm tasting something delicious," her mother says, working the flavors in her mouth. "Ginger, soy, oh, and baby corn. Where did you find fresh baby corn?"

She has something to say about everything. "Such sharp greens. Olives, what an idea, so Greek. The color of this pepper is fabulous. Red food is very good for you, high in something." She gobbles. "Eating is such a pleasure when you don't have to cook."

"Did you take care of your errands?" her father asks Ray.

"Yes, thank you," Ray says. "Every now and then it helps to use a car. I filled it with gas."

"You didn't need to."

"And I put a quart of oil in. I also checked the tires; your right rear was down a little."

"Thanks, Ray."

She hates him. She absolutely hates him. He is too good. How does a person get to be so good? She wishes she could get behind it, she wishes she could think he was as wonderful as he seems. But she doesn't trust him for a minute.

"More," her mother says, holding her plate up for seconds. "What's the matter—you're not eating?"

She shakes her head. If Ray is poisoning them, putting a little bit of who knows what into the food, she wants none of it. "Not hungry."

"I thought you said you were starving."

She doesn't answer.

"White rice and brown," her mother says. "Ray is kinder than I could ever be. I would never make two rices."

"Two rices make two people happy—that's easy," Ray says.

Her mother eats and then gets up from the table, letting her napkin fall into her plate. "That was wonderful—divine." She walks out of the room.

It takes her father longer to finish. "Great, Ray, really great." He helps clear the table.

She is left alone with Ray.

"Marriage is a difficult thing," Ray says without warning. She wonders whom he is talking about and if he knows more. "I was married once." He hands her a pot to dry. "Attachment to broken things is not good for the self."

"Is that where you got to be such a good cook? You're really something, a regular Galloping Gourmet."

"To feed yourself well is a strong skill." He speaks as though talking in translation.

"Where are you from, Ray?"

"Philadelphia."

She is thinking Main Line, that would explain it. Maybe that's why he doesn't care about anything, maybe money means nothing to him, because he already has it, because if he needs it, there is always enough.

"And what did your family do in Philadelphia?"

"They were in business."

"What sort of business?" she asks.

"Dresses," he says.

Not Main Line. "Do you have many friends in the area?"

He shakes his head. "I am not so easy, I don't like everybody."

"Do you have a family?" she asks.

"I have myself," he says.

"And what do you want from us?"

"You and I have only just met."

"My parents are very generous, simple people," she says. It sounds as though she's making him a deal, an offer. She stops. "I noticed you on the floor with the cymbals. Are you a guru, a swami of some sort?"

"I have been sitting for many years; it does me good, just noticing what I feel."

She is noticing that she feels like hitting him, hauling off and slugging him. The unrelenting evenness of his tone, his lack of interest in her investigation, his detachment is arrogant, infuriating. She wants to say, I've got your number; you think you're something special, like you were sent here from some other place, with little cymbals on your fingers—*ping*.

She wants to say, pretending you're so carefree, so absent of emotion, isn't going to get you anywhere—*ping*.

"Do not mistake me," he says, as though reading her mind. "My detachment is not arrogance, it is hard won."

If she hits him, he will not defend himself—she knows that. He will let her hit him; she will look like an idiot, it will look like proof of how crazy she is, it will look as though he did nothing to provoke her.

"This is just what you think of me," he says, nodding knowingly. "I am not anything. I am just here. I am not trying to go anywhere."

"I'm watching you," she says, walking out of the kitchen.

The door to her parents' room is closed. She knocks before entering. Her parents are sitting on the bed, reading.

"We're spending some time alone together," her mother says.

"Should I not bother you?"

"It's okay—you're not here very often," her mother says.

"What's Ray doing?" her father asks.

"Rearranging the shelves in the kitchen, throwing clay pots and firing them in the oven, and koshering chickens for tomorrow."

"What makes you always think everyone else is getting more than you?" her mother asks.

"You're hiding in your bedroom with the door closed and he's out there—loose in the house, doing God knows what. He's completely taken over, he's running the show, don't you see?"

"We're not hiding, we're spending time alone together."

She sneezes four times in quick succession. "Cat," she says.

"Did you bring anything to help yourself?"

"What the hell makes him so special that he gets to come and live here with his cat?"

"There's no reason not to share. In fact it's better, more economical, and he's very considerate," her father says. "If more people invited people in, it would solve the housing shortage, use less natural resources. We're just two people. What do we need a whole house for? It was my idea."

"Why don't you just open a shelter, take in homeless people and offer them free showers, et cetera?"

"Don't go completely crazy," her mother says. "There are no homeless people in Chevy Chase."

She looks around the room. "What happened to Grandma's table? It used to be in that corner."

"Mini-storage," her mother says. "We put a lot of things into storage."

"Boxes and boxes. We loaded a van and they took it all away."

"The house feels better now, doesn't it? Airier, almost like it's glad to be rid of all that crap," her mother says.

"Where is this mini-storage?" she asks.

"Somewhere in Rockville. Ray found it. Ray took care of the whole thing."

"Have you ever been there? How do you know your stuff is really there?" She is thinking she's figured it out, she finally has something on Ray.

"I have the key," her mother says. "And Ray made an inventory."

"Fine, first thing in the morning I'm going there. We'll see what's what."

"Why are you so suspicious? Your father doesn't have many friends, this is nice for him, don't ruin it."

"What do you even know about Ray—who is he really?"

"He writes," her father says.

"Yeah, he keeps a journal, I saw it downstairs."

"You shouldn't be poking around in his room," her mother says. "That's invasion of privacy."

"He's written five books, he's had stories in the *New Yorker*," her father says.

"If he's a world-famous writer, why is he living with you?"

"He likes us," her father says. "We're common travelers."

"We should all be so lucky to have someone willing to pay a little attention to us when we're old—it's not like you're going to move home and take care of us."

"I came home because I wanted you to take care of me. Steve and I are having a hard time. I think Steve may move out."

"You have to learn to leave people alone, you can't hound someone every minute. Maybe if you left him alone he'd come back." Her mother pauses. "Do you want Ray to go back with you?"

"And do what, help Steve pack?"

"He could keep you company. I'm not sure he's ever been to New York. He likes adventures."

"Mom, I don't need Ray. If I needed anyone, it would be you."

"No," her mother says. Simply no. She hears it and knows that all along the answer was no.

Her bedroom is simultaneously big and small. She is too big for the bed and yet feels like a child, intruding on her own life.

She pulls the shade and undresses. The night-light is on, it goes on automatically at dusk. She lies in the twin bed of her youth, looking at the bookcase, at the bear whose fur she tried to style, at her glass piggy bank still filled with change, at a *Jefferson Airplane—White Rabbit* poster clinging to the wall behind the dresser.

Stopped time. She is in both the past and present, wondering how she got from there to here. The mattress is hard as a rock. She rolls over and back. There is nowhere to go. She takes a couple of the new pills—Products for Modern Living.

She dreams.

Her mother and father are standing in the front hall with old-fashioned American Tourister suitcases.

"I'm taking your mother to Europe," her father says. "Ray is going to keep an eye on the house, he's going to take care of the dog."

"He's lonely," her mother says. "He came for coffee and brought us a cat."

She is hiding in the woods behind the house, watching the house with X-ray specs. Everything is black and white. She calls her brother from a walkie-talkie. "Are you out there? Can you hear me? Come in, come in?"

"Roger. I am here in sunny California."

"I'm watching Ray," she says.

"The mail just came," he says. "Ray sent me a birthday card and a hundred dollars in cash. That's more than Mom and Dad ever gave me."

"Do you know where Mom and Dad are?"

"I have no idea," he says. "They didn't even send a card."

And then Ray is chasing her around the yard with the cymbals on his fingers. Every time he punches his fingers together—*ping*—she feels a sharp electric shock. Her X-ray specs fall off. Everything changes from black-and-white to color.

Ray runs into the house and closes the door. The deadbolt slips into place.

She is on the other side of the glass. "Open the door, Ray."

She finds the key hidden under the pot. She tries it. The key doesn't work—Ray has changed the locks.

"Ray," she says, banging on the glass. "Ray, what have you done to my parents? Ray, I'm going to call the police."

"They're in Italy," Ray says, muffled through the glass.

She is on the walkie-talkie, trying to reach her mother in Italy.

"You're not understanding what I'm saying," she says. "Ray stole the house. He changed the locks. I can't get in."

"You don't have to yell, I'm not deaf," her mother says.

She wakes up. The house is silent except for two loud, sawing snores—her parents.

In the morning, she dresses in her room. With Ray in the house, she feels uncomfortable making the dash from the bedroom to the bathroom in her underwear. She gets dressed, goes to wash her face and pee, and then heads down the hall to the kitchen.

"Good morning," she says.

Ray is alone at the kitchen table.

"Where is everybody?"

"Your father had an art class and your mother went shopping with Mrs. Harris. She left you her car and the key for the mini-storage."

Ray holds up a string, dangling from it is a small key. He swings it back and forth hypnotically. "I'll give you directions," he says.

She nods.

"Would you like some herb tea? I just made a pot."

"No thanks." They sit in silence. "I'm not exactly a morning person," she says.

As she steps outside, Mrs. Lasky is across the way, getting into her car.

"How are you?" Mrs. Lasky calls out. "How is life in New York?"

"It's fine. It's fine." She repeats herself, having nothing more to say. "And how are you?"

"Very well," Mrs. Lasky says. "Isn't Ray wonderful? He keeps my bird feeder full. The most wonderful birds visit me. Just now, as I was having my breakfast, a female cardinal was having hers."

The mini-storage facility is called U-Store It. "U-store it. U-keep the key. U-are in charge." She locates the unit, unlocks the padlock, and pulls the door open.

There was something vaguely menacing about the way Ray was swinging the key through the air—yet he drew the map, he seemed not to know or care what she was thinking.

A clipboard hangs from a hook by the door. There is spare twine, tape, and a roll of bubble wrap. She recognizes the outlines of her grandmother's table, her father's old rocking chair. Each box is labeled, each piece of furniture well wrapped. On the clipboard is a typed list of boxes with appendices itemizing the contents of each box: Children's Toys, Mother's Dishes, World Book Encyclopedia A–Z (Plus YearBook 1960–1974), Assorted From Kitchen Closet, Beach Supplies, etc. She pries open a box just to be sure. She's thinking she might find wadded up newspaper, proof Ray is stealing, but instead, she finds her book reports from high school, a Valentine card her brother made for her mother, the hat her grandmother wore to her mother's wedding.

She seals the box up again. There is nothing to see. She pulls the door closed, locks it, and leaves.

Driving home, she passes her old high school—it's been gutted. BUILDING A BETTER FUTURE FOR TOMORROW'S LEADERS. READY FOR RE-OCCUPANCY FALL 2002. GO BARONS.

She drives up and down the streets, playing a nostalgic game of who lived where and what she can remember about them: the girl with the wonderful singing voice who ended up having to be extricated from a cult, the boy who in sixth grade had his own subscription to *Playboy,* the girl whose mother had Siamese twins. She remembers her paper route, she remembers selling Girl Scout cookies door to door, birthday parties, roller skating, Ice Capades.

She goes home.

Every time she comes to visit, it takes twenty-four hours to get used to things and then everything seems less strange, more familiar, everything seems as though it could be no other way—entirely natural.

She slides the car into the driveway. Her father is in the front yard, raking leaves. His back is toward her. She beeps, he waves. For a million years her father has been in the front yard, raking. He has his plaid cap on, his old red cardigan, and corduroys.

She gets out of the car.

"Remember when I was little," she calls down the hill. "And we used to rake together. You had the big one and I had the small bamboo . . ."

He turns. A terrifying sensation sweeps through her. It's Ray.

"I want you out," she says, shocked. "Now!" He intentionally misled her. He had to have known what she was thinking when she drove in, when she beeped and waved, when she said, remember when I was little. Why didn't he take off the hat, turn around, and say, I am not who you think I am?

"Where is my father? What have you done to my father? Those are not your clothes."

"Your father gave them to me."

She moves toward him.

Ray is standing there, her father's cap still on his head. She reaches out, she knocks it off. He bends to pick it up.

"It's not your hat," she says, grabbing it, throwing it like a Frisbee across the yard. "You can't just step inside someone's life and pretend you're them."

"I was invited."

"Get your stuff and get out."

"I'm not sure it's entirely up to you," Ray says. This is as close as he comes to protesting. "It's not your house."

"Oh, but it is," she says. "It's my house and it's my family and I have to have some influence on what happens here. They're old, Ray. Pick on someone else." She grabs the rake and uses it to shoo him inside. "It's over. Pack your bags."

Her mother comes home just as Ray is trying to put the cat into his travel case. The cat is screaming, howling. The cab is waiting outside.

"What's going on? Did something happen to the cat? Does he need me to take him to the vet?"

"He can't stay," she says. "He was in the yard acting like Daddy, he was wearing Daddy's clothes. He can't do that."

"He's your father's friend. We like having him here."

"He can't stay," she repeats.

"Maybe you shouldn't have come home," her mother says. "Maybe it's too hard. You know what they say."

"I'm just visiting," she says.

Ray comes up the stairs. He has a single suitcase, the cat carrier, and a brown paper bag filled with his supplements, his wheat germ, and the red and the green stuff.

"It doesn't have to be this way," her mother says.

"It does," she says.

"Good-bye," Ray says, shaking her mother's hand.

There's something about his shaking her mother's hand that's more upsetting than anything, it's heartbreaking and pathetic, it's more and less affecting than a clinging hug.

"Don't forget us, Ray," her mother says, walking him to the door, letting him out almost as easily as they let him in. "I'm so sorry, I apologize for the confusion."

And then he is gone. She goes down to his room. She checks the doors. He has left his key on the bed along with her father's clothes, neatly folded, his bedding all rolled up.

She comes back upstairs.

"Now what, Mrs. Big Shot?" her mother says. "Now who's going to take care of us?"

"I don't know."

"Your father didn't even have a chance to say good-bye."

"I'm not saying they can't be friends—I'm sure he'll see him at the next vitamin meeting—just that Ray can't live here. This isn't a commune."

She is sitting in the den. Her mother is knitting.

Her father comes home. "I made a nice drawing today," her father says.

"That's nice," her mother says.

"Were there any messages?"

"No," her mother says.

They sit in silence for a few minutes longer.

"Where's Ray?"

"She made him leave," her mother says, gesturing toward her with a knitting needle.

"He was in the yard, raking. He had your clothes on. I thought he was you—he scared me."

"He did a good job," her father says. "The yard looks good."

Again there is silence.

"Where'd he go?" her father asks.

"I have no idea, it all happened so quickly. Maybe back to the vitamin store," her mother says.

She feels as though she can't stay. She has shaken things up too much, she is really on the outside now.

"I guess I should go," she says.

Later that night she will take the train back to New York. The apartment will be empty. There will be a note from Steve. "I thought I should go. If you need me I'm at Bill's. Hope you had a good weekend."

"You come home, upset everything, and then you just leave?" her mother says. "What's the point of that?"

"I wanted to talk to you," she says.

"So talk," her mother says.

ROCKETS ROUND THE MOON

We were the boys of summer vacation, Henry Heffilfinger and me. It was my fifth summer at my father's house, six years after my parents divorced, three years after my mother remarried, the summer of '79, the summer I was twelve, the summer the world almost stopped spinning round.

Henry's mother picked me up at the airport. "Hello! Hello!" she called from the far end of the terminal, waving her arms through air, as if simultaneously fanning herself and guiding me in for landing.

"Oh, you look tall," she said, trying to wrestle away my carry-on bag. "Your father was busy; he asked me to come. So, that's why I'm here." She stopped for a minute, combed the hair out of my face with her fingernails. "We're so glad you've arrived; we're going to have a fine summer."

For that moment, while her pink frosted nails were tickling my skull, I believed her.

Luggage spun on a wide stainless-steel rack; suitcases slid up, down, sideways, crashing into each other with the painless thud of bumper cars. We stood watching until everything had come and gone, until there was nothing left except a couple of old bags that probably belonged to someone who'd died in a plane crash, who'd left their luggage forever going round and round.

"Where's Henry?" I asked.

Maybe Henry was my hero, maybe just my friend, I don't

know. He had a mother, a father, and a little sister, all together, on one street, in one city. He had no secrets.

"Guarding the car. I'm parked in a terrible place."

While I stood by the carousel, hoping my suitcases would home in and find me, Mrs. Henry took my luggage checks and went off in search of information.

If you're wondering what the point is calling Henry by his own name and then calling his mother Mrs. Henry, well what can I say, all the Heffilfingers were Henrys to me. Mr., Mrs., baby June, and Henry himself.

I rolled my eyes in a full circle counting the brown-and-yellow spots that made up the tortoiseshell rims of my glasses. They were new glasses, my first glasses. No one in Philly had seen them yet except Mrs. Henry, and she was sharp enough not to say anything.

A couple of months ago my school borrowed vision machines from the motor vehicle department and lined us all up. I looked into the viewfinder and said to the school nurse, "I can't see anything, it's pure blackness."

"Press your head to the bar, wise guy," she said.

I pressed my forehead against the machine and the screen lit up, but all that light still didn't do much good. The nurse sent me home with a note for my mother who simply said, "You're not getting contacts; you're too young and too irresponsible."

I thought of not taking the glasses to Philly, of going through one more blind, blurry summer, but the fact was they made a real difference, so I wore them, and kept the unbreakable case and a thousand specially treated cleaning sheets jammed into my carry-on bag.

Four-eyed, but alone in the Philadelphia airport, I may as well have been a boy without a brain. Like a sugar doughnut, I was glazed. Stiff.

It was the day after school ended. My mother had put me on the plane with a list of instructions/directions for my father, written out longhand on three sheets of legal paper, stuffed into one of Dr. Frankle's embossed envelopes. I was to be returned on or by the twenty-first of August, in good time for the usual back-to-school alterations: haircut, fresh jeans, new sneakers, book bag. I was only just becoming aware of how much everything was the product of a negotiation or a fight.

"Let's find Henry," Mrs. Henry suggested.

Let's not, I thought.

We were at the age where just showing up was frightening. You never knew who or what you might meet, a twelve-foot giant with a voice like a tuba, or Howdy Doody himself. Without warning, a body could go into spasm, it could stretch itself out to a railroad tie, it could take someone familiar and make them a stranger. A whole other person could claim the name, address, phone number, and fingerprints of a friend. There was the possibility that in those ten missing months a new life had been created, one that intentionally bore no relation to the past.

"Don't worry, they'll find your luggage," Mrs. Henry said. "They'll check the airport in Boston and the next plane coming in, and when they've got it, they'll deliver it out to the house. You'll have it by suppertime. Let's go," she said. "Makes no sense to wait here."

The automatic doors popped open. Henry stood there, arms open, exasperated.

"What the hell is going on?" he screamed. "They're about to tow our car. They asked me for my license!"

Mrs. Henry turned red. She tugged on the strap of my shoulder bag. We ran forward.

"I've never heard of anything taking so long," Henry said when we got outside.

There was no tow truck. There was nothing except a long line of cars dropping off people, and men in red caps going back and forth from the cars to the terminal wheeling suitcases that weren't lost yet. There wasn't even a ticket on the Henrys' windshield.

And Henry wasn't a giant. He wasn't six feet tall, either. He was skinny, with shoulders that stuck straight out of him like the top of a T square.

"What happened?" he asked.

"The airline has misplaced your friend's luggage."

He turned to me, finally noticing I was there, I existed. "Why'd you get glasses?"

"Blind," I said.

Five years ago, before I ever met him, Henry was offered to me by my father as a kind of bribe.

"Philadelphia will be fun," my father had said. "We bought this house especially for you. There's a boy your age living next door; you can be best friends."

My first day there I stood three-foot-something, waiting smack in the middle of the treeless, flowerless, nearly grassless front yard as nonchalantly as a seven-year-old could. I knew no other way of announcing myself. When the sun had crossed well over its midday mark, when what seemed like years had passed, a station wagon pulled into the driveway just past me and the promised boy jumped out and without stopping ran toward the kitchen door of his house. The screen door opened, but instead of admitting him, a yellow-rubber-gloved hand pushed the boy out again. The body attached to the hand followed and Mrs. led Henry to the edge of their yard and nodded in my direction.

"Henry, this is your new friend. He's here for the whole summer," she said.

"Bye," Henry said, taking off again in the direction of the kitchen door, whipping open the screen, and vanishing into the house.

"You can't stand outside all summer, you'll be a regular Raisinette, go on, after him," Mrs. Henry said, clapping her hands.

The geography of the Henrys' house was the exact same

as my father's house, but theirs was more developed. The top floor had blue carpet; the middle level, yellow; and the lower level was green. The sky, the sun, the lawn. It made perfect sense. It was beautiful. Everywhere I'd ever lived the floors were wooden or carpeted a neat and dull beige or gray. Here I had the sensation of floating, skimming through the rooms like a hovercraft. I went through the house, stunned by the strangeness of being alone among the lives of others.

I found Henry on the lower level setting up a Parcheesi board.

"Do you know how to play or do I have to teach you?"

"I know how," I said.

"That's a relief. You don't look like you know anything."

I didn't answer.

"Can you swim?"

I nodded.

"Tomorrow we'll go to the pool."

He hurled a series of questions at me like rockets, little hand grenades. I ducked and bobbed; I answered as best I could. It was a test, an application for friendship.

"I'm allowed to go off the diving board but I don't like it," he said. "But I don't tell anyone that. If someone is going, I go too, but it's nothing I'm in a rush to do. You first," he said, dropping the dice into my hand. I started to shake them. He immediately stopped me.

"We don't play that way," he said. "You go like this." Between his thumb and forefinger, he held one up in the air then dropped it with a whirling twist. Before the first one stopped spinning, he dropped the second one the same way. The dice splashed down onto the board, knocking over my marker, giving me a six and a four. "See," he said, moving my marker for me. "It's better that way."

"I should go home," I said when the game was over, when he'd played the whole thing for both of us, when I'd never touched the marker or the dice.

"Are you sure you wouldn't like to have a snack?" Mrs. asked me as I headed for the screen door. "I made cream-filled cupcakes."

"The ones with white stuff inside," Henry said.

"You can make cupcakes like that?"

"Yes." She smiled at me.

Every year just as I started to have a sense of how things were laid out, of where Philadelphia started and stopped, it was time for me to leave. The Henrys' car wound down the streets with me pressed to the window, wondering where the hell we were.

"Where's baby June?" I asked, my twelve-year-old voice cracking with what I thought was middle age or Parkinson's disease.

"Day camp," Mrs. Henry said.

Baby June's real name was Constance, but since her mission in life appeared to be a well-studied imitation of Mrs., everyone except Mrs. and Mr. called her baby June.

Henry and I were quiet. There was the familiar awkwardness of beginning again, of seeing a body once more after months away. In between, we'd talked a couple of times, signed our names to birthday cards picked out by mothers in a hurry, we'd given the okay to a present we knew would be perfect only because we wanted it so bad for ourselves. But that was about it.

"You'd better check in," Mrs. said when we pulled into the driveway. "Then come over for lunch. We'll be waiting."

"You'll be waiting," Henry said, slamming the car door. "I'm eating now."

Except for the hum of the air-conditioning, which was running even though it was only seventy-some degrees out, my father's house was without signs of life.

I left my carry-on in the hall and called my mother. Dr. Frankle answered the phone. I didn't tell him his luggage was missing.

"Is my mother there?"

"She's on the Lifecycle," he said, and then there was silence.

"Could I talk to her please?"

"I'll have to get the cordless."

"Thank you," I said. There was the longest silence, as though Dr. F. thought if he waited long enough to get my mother, I'd grow up and be gone.

"You're there," my mother said, out of breath.

"I'm here."

"That was fast."

"They can't find my suitcase."

"Don't worry, they will," she said. "They have to. Did your father pick you up?"

"No. Mrs. Henry did it."

"What the hell's wrong with him. That's part of our agreement."

"I don't know," I said.

"Have you spoken to him?"

"I called you first."

"When you talk to him, tell him to call me right away. That's all. I'll deal with him. I don't want to drag you into this."

"What if my stuff doesn't show up?"

"Your father will take care of it," she said.

According to all reports—except my own—by marrying Dr. Frankle, my mother had done well for herself. On the other hand, my father seemed to have taken a small financial slide. Even though Dr. F. could more than cover the world with money, my father still sent my mother a check every month, supposedly for me.

"Did they leave you lunch?" my mother asked.

"I've been invited out."

"Well, have fun. I'll talk to you Saturday morning before my hair appointment. If you need anything just call." I could hear air rushing through the sprockets of the Lifecycle.

My father answered his own phone at the office. "Hi ya, sport. Get in okay?"

"My suitcase is temporarily dislocated."

"Happens all the time."

"Mom wants you to call her."

"Why?"

"I don't know," I said, lying.

"Well, I gotta get to work," he said. "There should be something there for lunch if you're hungry."

"I'm invited to the Henrys'."

"Oh, that's good. Well, run along. Don't keep people waiting. And don't forget, Cindy's making dinner tonight."

"Great."

Every year Cindy made dinner my first night in town. "A real dinner," she called it: sitting down, plates, glasses, a meatlike item, strange salad—one year with flower petals in it—doctored brown rice, and herbal iced tea. After that, for the rest of the summer, eating was pretty much something I took care of at the Henrys', where they seemed to have a firmer grasp of what was food and what was indigenous vegetation, animal habitat, something to be seen, perhaps cut and put in a vase, but certainly not eaten. Sometimes, I'd ride to the grocery store with Mrs. and buy real food, making sure to get enough for my father and Cindy, who ultimately ate more crap than anyone.

Cindy was ten years younger than my dad, and all they'd talked about when they bought this place was how great it was for kids. For these five years, I'd felt the burden of making that seem true.

"He shops," I once overheard Cindy tell someone. "And he's such a pleasure to have around."

A pleasure because I was hardly around. Plus, I was household-oriented. I liked things clean and neat. I found comfort in order. I was also used to being around people I didn't know, living with people I wasn't related to. I kept my own secrets. I'd taught myself to be a little less than human.

I'd taught myself to be a person whom people like to have around, half boy, half butler: half, just half—no one wanted the whole thing, that was one of the tricks, if you wanna call it that.

I pulled the box of chocolate I'd brought for Mrs. H. out of my carry-on. I'd picked liquor-filled, thinking it was safer than milk chocolate in terms of keeping it from Henry and baby June. Liquor-filled tasted so foul that only an adult would eat it. I washed my hands and face and set out for the Henrys'.

Lunch was like something out of a commercial or a dream, although I suppose there was nothing unusual about it. Baloney-and-cheese sandwiches on white bread—mayo on one side, mustard on the other, and pale pink meat and yellow cheese in the middle. Heaven. In Dr. Frankle's house the only baloney was verbal, and in my father's the only meat was a soy-based pseudohamburger mix called bean-burger.

"Chips?" Mrs. Henry asked.

"Yes, please." Real chips, not extra crispy, gourmet deep-bake-fried, slightly, lightly not salted. Normal American chips out of a big old bag-o'-chips. I was glowing. Orange drink. Not orange juice, but drink. It may as well have been a birthday party. Henry didn't notice, he didn't care, he didn't appreciate anything.

Mrs. H. topped off my glass. My tongue would be orange all day; if I sucked on it hard, I'd be able to pull out little flashes of flavor for hours to come.

"I'm so glad to be here," I said, meaning it completely.

"We've missed you," Mrs. said.

"I haven't," Henry said. "I've been busy."

"Oh, Henry, you sit in the house, whining all the time, 'I'm bored. There's nothing to do.'"

"TV is your best friend," I said.

"No, yours," Henry said.

"No," I said. "Yours. We don't have a TV."

"God, how depressing," Henry said.

There was a moment of silence while everyone—even Mrs. H.—reflected on the idea of life without television.

"That was great, thank you," I said to Mrs. when we were finished.

"It was baloney," Henry said.

I carried the plates to the sink.

"You're so considerate," Mrs. said, staring Henry down.

I try, I said to myself. I try so hard.

"Come on," Henry said. "Hurry up." He pushed me out the screen door.

From the edge of their backyard, if I listened hard, I could hear the deceiving rush that five years ago I thought was water. From the end of this block that went nowhere—dead-ended three houses away into a thick wood—I'd heard a clean whooshing sound that I thought was a lot of water. A waterfall maybe. A paradise on the other side of something. An escape from the starkness of this street. Before I knew better, I went charging off into fifteen feet of thick woods, the kind of woods bogeymen come from, woods where little kids playing find a human hand poking through the leaves, the nails long from the inattentions of the not-so-recently dead, the kind of place where animals crawl off to die. I punched my way through only to find that what whooshed and roared was an eight-lane highway where a hundred thousand cars sliding by in both directions had the nerve to sound like a waterfall. Hearing it again on this first afternoon depressed me.

"Give me your glasses," Henry said, kneeling down.

I handed them over, imagining Henry slipping the frames under the ball of his foot, and then leaning full forward, laughing at the snap-crackle-pop sound of two hundred and fifty dollars shattering.

"They're very expensive," I said.

"I'm not buying them."

He used the glasses to catch the sun and burn holes through an old dead leaf.

"Handy," he said, giving them back to me. "I guess you can keep them." He stopped for a second, then looked at me. "So, what's wrong with you, how come you're not talking? Brain go blind, too?"

"Trip," I said. "I don't like to fly."

"Wouldn't know," Henry said. "Pool's open. We can go tomorrow."

In Philadelphia there was a community pool, long and wide. All you had to do was show up and sign in. Henry and I ruled it in the summer. We never took showers before entering. We stepped over the vat of milky green below the sign ALL BATHERS MUST IMMERSE FEET BEFORE ENTERING WATER. Whatever disease we might have had, we thought it better than the lack of disease we saw around us, we wanted to infect everyone, anyone, we wanted everything about ourselves to be contagious, we were dying for someone to be just like us. We were the boys who only got out of the water when the guard blew his whistle fifteen minutes before the hour—every hour—and announced, "Adult swim. Eighteen and under out of the pool." Those words were mystical, almost magical. We'd crawl out and sit by the edge watching, as if adult swim meant that the pool would become pornographic for those fifteen very adult minutes just before the hour. But nothing ever happened. The only pornography were the old women with breasts big enough to feed a nation and old men with personal business hanging so far down that it sometimes fell out the end of their bathing suits.

Every day we stayed at the pool until Henry's mother called the office and had us paged and ordered home. Then waterlogged, bloody-eyed, bellies bloated from the ingestion of too much chlorinated water, cheap snack-bar pizza, and too many Milky Ways, we walked home, wet towels around our necks, our little generals shriveled, clammy, and chafing under our cutoffs. We bore it all proudly, as though it were the most modern medical treatment, the prescription guarantee for a better life, a bright manhood. Our flip-flops slippery wet, heels sliding off and into the dirt, strange evening bugs and twigs snapping at our ankles, we wound down the long hill onto the road, and then across the road, through some yards, through the short woods between developments toward the light in the Henrys' kitchen window.

As the days stretched out to full length, Mrs. Henry always started talking about where she wanted to spend her summer vacation, two golden weeks she'd suffered the year for. She'd talk about going to Rome to see the pope or to Venice to ride in a gondola or even off to Australia to see koala bears, but in the end the Henrys always ended up going somewhere like the nearest beach, toting me along because it was easier to bring an extra kid to entertain Henry than to try to do it themselves.

In the evenings, after dinner, Mrs. Henry went out onto the new wooden deck that Mr. had built over the old slab-o'-concrete porch. While baby June played with her dolls, Mrs. Henry sat back on a lounger holding a tall glass of diet soda, filled with ice cubes melted down into hailstones. Every now and then, she'd shake the drink, mix it up, and say, "Brings the carbonation to life."

As soon as the weather got warm and everyone started running in and out of the new sliding glass door, Mrs. Henry went to the hardware store, bought a roll of glow-in-the-dark orange tape, and made a huge safety star on the glass door, top to bottom, to remind everyone not to go charging through.

"I don't want anyone ending up with a face full of glass, stitches, scars, and disfigurement. I'd feel terrible."

It worked. We all felt careful and safe. Mrs. H. sat out there resting with baby June while Henry and I played badminton in the yard. *Shuttlecock.* We loved that word. We said it loudly and brightly a thousand times a day for absolutely no reason. We'd go down to Woolworth's and loudly ask each other, "You don't think they'd have shuttlecocks here, do you?" The shuttlecock would go up high in the air, its red

rubber end obscene, wonderful, and probably the only reason we played the game. The cock would rise into the last
moment of light and then sink into the darkness of the Penn-
sylvania backyard, dropping softly onto the grass.

Deep at the farthest end of the yard, round, multicolored
plastic lights bobbed up and down on the back fence. The
lights had been up every one of my Philadelphia years, as
though the Henrys' life were a never-ending tropical party, as
if they were the happiest people in the world. Sometimes the
lights were like buoys. Henry and I would lie out on the deck
pretending we were at sea. Depending on our mood, the
lights were beacons, telling us how to steer, how to avoid
dangerous straits and shipwrecks of summers past. Other
times they were other yachts filled with wonderful and
famous people. We'd stand on the bow, waving. We'd look
through Henry's binoculars into the dead black of night and
pretend we were seeing all manner of decadent behavior. In
detail, we'd describe it to each other.

One afternoon, later that summer, Mrs. Henry started
gliding around the kitchen in a definite rhythm—one-two-
three: refrigerator-sink-stove—as though cooking were dancing, as though she could waltz with hamburgers.

Tiny grease balls spattered and popped in the frying pan,
shooting off into the gas flames where they exploded into
miniature blue-and-orange fireballs of fat, cheap summer
sparklers. The hamburgers were almost done. I usually didn't
pay this much attention to the state of dinner, especially dinner that wasn't really my own, but I happened to be in the
middle of a growth spurt or something and was on the verge
of starvation. My stomach was puffing out, and I was having
difficulty concentrating on anything other than the six
hockey pucks of beef sizzling not a body's length away, wondering how the six pucks would be divided among four,
hopefully five, people.

Voluntarily, I set the table, pretending not to be anything other than a good neighbor, a nice boy.

Mrs. turned from the stove to a dying head of lettuce.

"Where is he?" she said, referring to Mr. Henry. "I hate it when he does this. Dinner's almost ready. We're going to have to eat."

She raised the frying pan up off the fire. The phone rang and rang again. She answered it. "I'm sorry, what?" she said, using her chin to pull the phone closer to her ear. She held the pan above the stove, slightly tilted. The hamburgers stopped sizzling. "No," she said. "No, I don't think that's right."

Without realizing what she was doing, she pushed the frying pan forward, threw it down in the sink, which was more than six inches deep with dirty water, dead lettuce, and mixed vegetable scraps.

Henry screamed, "No."

The burgers landed with one great searing hiss, immediately sank, and neither Henry nor I could figure a rescue plan fast enough.

Six burgers a goner was all I could think. I could tell Henry was furious. His top lip had disappeared into a thin white line of pure Henry fury.

"I'm going to give you ten dollars to keep an eye on Constance for a couple of hours. Don't use the stove or the oven. You can microwave." She turned off the gas, picked up her purse, and went out the door. "That's our dinner," Henry said, pointing to the handle of the frying pan poking up. A single burger had risen and was somehow skimming the surface of the muck looking less like food than the final result of eating. "It's gross, I'm not touching it."

We went through the cabinets, found a box of macaroni-and-cheese mix, bright orange and gooey. Later, it made my stomach turn.

"I'm hungry," Henry said after the neon glop was gone.

"Would you like me to make you something?" baby June said, dragging her Easy-Bake out of the kitchen closet.

"Oh, I wanna cake baked by a lightbulb," Henry said. "That sounds wonderful, a gourmet treat."

"You do?" She lit up like she was the electricity that would power the bulb. "Isn't it wonderful," she said, patting the oven. "What kind do you want? Yellow or black?"

"It's yellow or chocolate," I said.

Baby June shrugged. She didn't care. She baked us each a cake and then delivered them as though waiting on us was the greatest thing in the world. We thought she was nuts.

"You want a real toy?" Henry asked her. Baby June nodded. He went deep into his closet and pulled out an old toy machine gun. "It still works," he said.

Baby June took the gun, raised the barrel to her eye, looked inside, and simultaneously pulled the trigger, shooting herself in the face, no joke.

"I don't get it," she said. "It doesn't do anything except make noise."

"It kills people," Henry said.

"Oh."

Mrs. arrived home hours later, white as rice. She locked the sliding glass door, the front door, and turned out the lights while Henry, baby June, and I sat silenced by her strangeness in the sudden dark of their living room. We watched her go wordlessly up the stairs and heard the bedroom door shut.

"The hamburgers are still in the sink," I said to Henry, who didn't get it. "Your mother has never gone to bed leaving the kitchen dirty. She doesn't do that. She always wipes a damp sponge across the counters, turns off the light over the stove, and wraps her dishrag through the refrigerator handle before going upstairs."

"What are you?" Henry asked. "A pervert?"

I didn't answer.

"Six burgers are drowned," I said, emphasizing the sinking sensation of the word *drowned.*

Henry went up the stairs, stood outside the door of his

parents' room, and said in a loud, demanding voice, "When's Dad coming home?"

"Sometime tomorrow" was the muffled answer.

The fact that she'd answered at all compelled Henry to push the questioning further.

"Are you getting a divorce?" he asked in a loud booming word-by-word voice you'd use to speak in the face of a tidal wave.

From the bottom of the steps, I saw Mrs. open the door in her robe.

"This isn't about Daddy and me," she said. "Your father had a problem with the car. He's trying to straighten things out."

"There are dishes in the sink—it's gross."

Mrs. adjusted her hair, pulled her robe tighter, put one fuzzy pink slipper in front of the other, and marched into the kitchen. She snapped on her rubber gloves, reached deep into the muck, pulled out the macaroni dishes, the frying pan, and, one by one, with the expression of a woman changing diapers, plucked hamburger after hamburger out of the water, held each up in the air for a few seconds to drain, and then dropped the remains into a trash can. She brushed her hair back with her elbow, shook Comet over everything, and went to work under hot water. The steam and Comet mixed to form a delicious noxious cloud-o'-cleanliness that drifted through the house. Whatever had happened hours earlier, the moment that caused dinner to drown, had been a kind of lapse, a seizure of sorts, but now with the green cellulose sponge in hand, everything was all right.

Mrs. Henry turned on the floodlight by the kitchen door, so I could see my way home. A three-foot path of white light cut through the darkness and lit up the grass green and bright.

There was a hill between the houses. A five-foot bump of dirt that changed things. The adults in either house didn't know each other well; it was too much work. To say hello they had to go around the long way, out the front door, down the flagstone blocks to the sidewalk, up the next driveway, up the flagstone blocks to the three steps, to the front door, and ring the doorbell, ring, ring. Hi, just thought I'd stop over. It didn't happen. If the land had been flat, if geography had been on their side, everything would have been easier. But the way it was, the Henrys were trapped. On the right edge of their property was a high homemade fence and on the left was this grass-covered tumor-o'-land that may as well have been Mount Baldy.

"Good night," I said and ran up the mountain toward the house on top of the hill. Mrs. turned the floodlight out behind me.

Using my key I opened the door to the house that would never be my own. The clock in the front hall banged out ten chimes.

My father and Cindy were sitting at the dining-room table, gnawing like rabbits on the remains of a huge salad— my father's evening grazing, as always, supplemented by a microwaved Lean Eating entrée, parked by his plate like someone's morning vitamin pill. Every night after their evening meal my father and Cindy disappeared into the "master bedroom suite." I could hear the click of the door locking. Buried in the "suite" was a custom-crafted tub big enough for six people, a cross-country ski machine, an exercise bike, VCR, twenty-six-inch TV, king-size bed, and even a small fridge. In case of nuclear attack, close bedroom door and wait for the next generation to save you.

What annoyed me the most was the locking of the door. Who did it? Cindy or my father? And how could they think that I, Mr. Privacy himself, was going to come busting in on them? It was infuriating. The other possibility was that they were really doing something in there, something I couldn't even begin to imagine, although I did imagine.

Alone, I did the dishes, mine and theirs, flipped through the mail, pretended to read the paper, and then, suffocating in boredom and frustration, turned on the eleven o'clock news.

"Early this afternoon, a Philadelphia boy was struck and killed by a car as he was crossing the street on his way home from a program for gifted and talented youth at Herbert Hoover Junior High. Thomas Stanton the Third, who had just turned thirteen earlier this week, was taken to University Hospital where he was pronounced dead. According to police reports, the car was traveling at substantial speed. The driver, forty-three-year-old John Heffilfinger, also of Philadelphia, was arrested at the scene." A picture of Mr. Henry flashed on the screen—Heffilfinger, no wonder I called them all Henrys—I truly almost didn't know who it was. I'd never seen him as anything other than Mr. Henry until that moment, when he was plucked out, taken from the Henrys, and put in a whole new category, John "Henry" Heffilfinger, Killer.

When Mr. Henry seemed to be late getting home, I didn't even think twice about it. Sometimes when fathers are late it's a good thing. Sometimes they're buying things, surprises you'd asked for but never thought you'd get—snorkel mask, fins, a better bike.

At thirteen, Thomas Stanton III had enough names and numbers behind his name to sound old enough and scary enough to run a bank. Poor Mr. H., was all I could think. Poor all the Hs. Did Henry even know? After turning out the floodlight behind me, did Mrs. call him into the kitchen for a long sit-down? Or was he alone up in his room, discovering this for himself on his private thirteen-inch Sony?

"Early this afternoon," the newscaster had said. It hadn't even happened at night, or at twilight when darkness and light mix together like spit in a kiss. It didn't happen at some forgivable moment when Mr. Henry could claim the sun at the horizon line blotted out everything, and he and the boy had dipped into darkness. In the middle of a perfectly good afternoon in the end of June, with a breeze that tickled the air like fingertips, he'd become a killer.

News travels fast. "Stay home today," my father said,

ducking his head into my room before he left for the office. "Mr. Heffilfinger has a problem and should be left alone."

I didn't say anything. After he and Cindy were gone, I got up, got dressed, ate breakfast, and sat looking out the front window at all the houses just like my father's, every single one pressed out of the same red brick Play-Doh mold. The ones across the street didn't come face to face, eye to eye, with ours, they looked into a small half court of their own. I saw those neighbors only in profile, coming and going, carrying bags of groceries up the sidewalk, watering the lawn, pounding a rug, or tending a failing barbecue. They were all Flat Stanleys. Human Colorforms, flat slices of bright, shiny, plastic laid down on a prepainted cardboard world—they could be peeled up and put down again and again, in any order or combination.

With nothing better to do and no options, I started putting wood-grain contact paper in all my dresser drawers. Halfway through, Henry rang the doorbell.

"Can I come in?"

I nodded and stepped back. Henry followed me upstairs to my room.

"I'm just gonna sit here," he said, patting the edge of my bed.

I didn't say anything. It was one of those times when clearly no one should talk. I finished cutting, peeling, laying the paper in the drawers, and then put my clean clothing back into the dresser much more slowly, more carefully than a normal person would. When I finished, and Henry still hadn't talked, I started cleaning, dusting, polishing, rearranging. I was on the verge of remodeling the whole house before he said anything.

"I guess you found out why dinner got wrecked," he said.
"Yeah."

"My father killed a kid," he said and then stopped. "I guess you know that," he said.

I nodded.

"That's why dinner got wrecked."

I nodded again and thought I'd never be able to eat hamburger again, macaroni and cheese, either. I'd end up becoming a vegetarian like my father and Cindy, eating rabbit-food dinners at midnight, then locking myself in my room.

"He's coming home this afternoon," Henry said. "Why? Why are they letting him out?"

He looked up at me; I looked away.

I shrugged and shrugged and shrugged, and Henry shrugged, and then finally we went downstairs, ate all the decent things we could find, and sat looking out the front window, waiting for Mr. Henry to be brought back.

I can't say Mr. Henry came home from the police station a different man. He was exactly the same the day after as he was the day before. There were no signs of him having snapped out of himself for the instant it took to kill, no indication that all the badness, the frustration, the lifetime buildup of a man's anger, had risen up through his gut, through his blood like a whirling dervish, like the man out of the Mr. Clean bottle, and that all the swirling whirlingness had forced his foot to the floor and hurled the car forward over Thomas Stanton III. I looked for that but saw nothing except dull gray around the eyes from too little sleep, too much fear, and stubble from a day's missed shaving.

"I'm being used," Henry said two days later as he was putting on the clothes his mother had laid out for him: gray pants, striped shirt, tie, blue jacket, hard shoes. The Henrys were going to court. A skinny lawyer with teeth so rotten they smelled bad had shown up the night before and explained to all the Henrys that they had to "dress up and put on a show, featuring Mr. Heffilfinger as father, provider, and protector."

In the hall all the Henrys went by, ducking in and out of the bedrooms, the bathroom. There was the hiss of aerosol spray, the dull whir of the hair dryer. All the running around and good clothes would have been festive if it wasn't ten A.M. on a weekday, liable to be the hottest day of the year so far, and if the destination weren't the county courthouse.

As soon as the lawyer pulled into the driveway, Mr. Henry went out, got into the back seat of his car, and closed the door. The rest of the Henrys were all downstairs, ready to go, except for Henry himself.

Mrs. Henry came upstairs. "We're ready to leave," she said.

Henry was lying down on the bed. He didn't move.

"Henry, we can't be late. Come on now."

Still nothing. His mother took his arm and began to pull. Henry pulled in the opposite direction.

"I don't want to fight with you," she said, leaning back, using her weight and position to good advantage. "It's for your father. Do this for your father."

Henry stopped resisting and was pulled off the bed and onto the floor.

"Stand up or you'll get dusty."

The lawyer came into his room. "Get up. We have to go."

Henry lay flat on the floor in his coat and tie. The back of the blue blazer picking up lint balls like it was designed to do that.

"I'm not going," Henry finally said.

"Oh yes you are," the lawyer said.

Together, the lawyer and Henry's mother lifted him to standing. I was sitting in the corner, in the old green corduroy chair that used to be in the living room. For the first time ever I felt like I didn't belong there, I felt like I was seeing something I shouldn't, something too private.

"Unless you plan on dragging me the whole way, leave me alone," Henry said to the lawyer.

The lawyer pushed him back onto the bed. "Do you want me to tell you something?"

Henry shook his head.

"If you don't sit in that courtroom and act right and if

your daddy gets sent to jail, I don't want you to ever forget that it might be your fault. Just because you felt like being a bogey little brat. Think on that," the lawyer said, checking his watch.

Henry looked at me, then stood and dusted himself off. Mrs. turned and went out of the room. Henry tipped his head toward the lawyer and said, "You're the biggest fucking asshole in the world."

The lawyer didn't respond except to look down at Henry like he wanted to kill him.

"And your fly is open, fuckwad," Henry said and then marched out of the room on his mother's heels, not staying to see the lawyer's face flush red, his hands grab at his crotch.

From Henry's bedroom window I watched the rest of them get into the lawyer's Lincoln. You could tell it was going to be the kind of day where the heat would raise people's tempers past the point of reconciliation. After they left, I left, pulling the door closed behind me and crossing the grass to wait in the air-conditioned silence of the house next door.

Later that afternoon, when I was back at the Henrys', their phone began to ring. It started slowly and then rang more and more, faster and faster, until it seemed to be ringing nonstop. Strangers, reporters, maniacs, guys Mr. had gone to junior high school with, lawyers offering to consider the case for a fee, someone from a TV show in New York City.

"You really should call the TV people back," Henry said to his parents.

"Stay away from it," Mrs. Henry said when the ringing started again. She held her arms down and out like airplane wings. "Don't touch."

"Are you going to work tomorrow?" Mrs. asked Mr.

"I don't know."

"Have you spoken to your office?"

"No," he said.

"You don't have to be afraid. Accidents happen," Mrs. said.

"You shouldn't say that," Mr. said.

Mrs. pointed her finger at Mr. "You have to stop acting like a guilty man," she said. "Did you wake up that morning and say to yourself, 'I'm going to kill a little boy today'?"

"I have blood on my shoes," Mr. shouted, "I feel like my feet are dripping in blood."

"It's your imagination," Mrs. said.

"I killed someone," he said, pushing his face close into Mrs.'s.

She pushed him away. "Stop acting insane."

Henry sat on baby June's swing set in the backyard, waiting for time to pass, for everything to return to normal, but Thomas Stanton III was ahead of Henry, six months ahead. He was already across the border of thirteen when he died, and he stayed there like a roadblock, a ton-o'-bricks, like all the weight in the world. Without seeming to know what he was doing, Henry started combing his hair that same certain way that Stanton's was in the newspaper photo. He started wearing clothes a gifted and talented type would wear: button-down shirts with a plastic pen protector in the pocket, pants a size too small. He started trying to look like a genius and ended up looking like a clown, like someone permanently dressed up for Halloween.

"Henry," I said, sitting facing him on the double horse swing. "It has to stop. You don't know what you're doing."

He brushed his hair back with a whole new gesture, just the way the dead kid would do it.

"Henry, you're making me hate you."

"Go home. Get your own life. Leave me alone," he said.

And so, with nothing else to do, with no other options, I did exactly that. I went to the pool alone.

Without Henry I was too intimidated to step over the pool of muck by the door. I dipped my feet in, and in a split second the milky white wash cauterized the summer's worth of cuts and scratches and I was sanitized for sure.

I unrolled my towel down on a lounger just at the edge of the tetherball court and next to a group of kids my own age. I watched a boy smack the ball so hard I could feel the stinging in my palms. The ball spun fast, its rope winding quick and high over the head of the other boy. I saw the smacker jump up and hit it again. The ball spun harder, faster, in tighter circles, until all the rope was wound and the stem of the ball itself smacked the pole, froze a second, and then slowly started to unwind.

"Thomas was my boyfriend," I overheard a skinny girl with blond hair hanging down the sides of her face like wet noodles say. "No one was supposed to know, but since he died, the secret came out. It was the single most horrifying experience of my life." She adjusted and readjusted the empty pink-and-white top of her bikini, pulling on the bottoms where they would have latched onto her butt if she'd had a butt. "The car stopped only after Thomas was sucked under and came out the other side, with grease smears down his body." She took a breath. "My mother tried to hold me back, but I touched him. 'Thomas,' I said. 'Thomas, can you hear me?' He lifted himself off the street and walked himself over to the grass, then crumpled like when you pull the middle out of a stack of things and it all falls down. He opened his mouth and a brown nutty thing they said later was his tongue fell out. 'Thomas,' my mother said. 'Thomas, everything is going to be all right. You've been in a little accident. These things can happen to anyone.'"

"What about the guy who did it?" the girl she was talking to asked.

"He sat in his car until the police came, and then jumped out and started to run. They chased after him and dragged him back so we could identify him."

"I don't think so," I said, interrupting, without even knowing what I was doing.

"What does that mean?" the girl asked.

"It was on TV," I said. "I don't think he tried to get away."

"So what if he didn't, what do you care," she said. "He wasn't your boyfriend. And you're not even from around here anyway."

I shrugged and looked evenly at her. Without a word, I got up. As I walked, the rough cement around the pool sanded the soles of my feet. At the edge of the water, I threw myself forward, hoping that when the water caught me, it would not be hard, it would not be icy cold, it would be enveloping like Jell-O. I broke the surface for air and went under again. Without Henry, with nothing to do, I swam laps, back and forth a thousand times.

Henry and I made up. We didn't talk about anything. He just came over to my house with new Ping-Pong paddles and said, "My mother bought me these, wanna play?" and I said, "Why not."

Two weeks to the day after the accident, while Mrs., Henry, and I were eating lunch—reheated tuna noodle casserole, with fresh chips crumbled on top, and green Gatorade—someone rang the doorbell and, without waiting for an answer, tried the knob.

Mrs. went to the kitchen door, cracked it open, and called, "Can I help you?" around the corner of the house.

"I've come about my son," the woman said. She stepped into the kitchen, opened her purse, pulled out a stack of papers, and with the palm of her hand spread them out into a messy fan on the kitchen table. Henry and I moved our plates back to give her more room. We held our napkins up to our mouths to hide our expressions.

"These are his report cards. He mostly got straight As except in spelling and music; he wasn't very good at music, couldn't carry a tune. This is his first school picture," she said, digging out a photo with three rows of kids, twenty-six young scrubbed faces, one kid holding a black sign with white lettering, HITHER HILLS ELEMENTARY SCHOOL, KINDERGARTEN. "We didn't buy his school picture this year. He said

115

he didn't like it. He thought his hair looked funny. Why didn't I just buy it anyway?" She was talking to herself. "Maybe if I'd taken the photo this wouldn't have happened. Why do I have these?" she asked, looking at Mrs. "What are they for? The insurance company wants me to calculate what he would have been worth if he'd had a life. I have to give them a figure. It's like playing *The Price Is Right*." She stopped for a minute, drew in a breath, and pressed the back of her hand against her eyes, blotting them. "You want to see how it feels, you want me to take one of yours?" She put her hand on Henry. "Christmas is coming," she said, even though it was July. "What will I do?"

The dead boy's mother stood crying in the Henrys' kitchen and when Henry's mother tried again to touch her, to comfort her, she wailed. Then, without a word, without a sound other than the swallowing of great gulps of air, she turned and walked out the kitchen door.

Henry's mother scooped up all the dead boy's report cards, prize certificates, letters from the governor for being on the honor roll, and handed them to me. "Go on, get her before she goes," she said.

I charged out the door, got to the lady before she got into her car, and said, "You forgot these."

"I didn't forget them," she said, again blotting her eyes with the back of her hand.

"Well, I'll put them in your car," I said. I went over to the passenger side, opened the door, and left them there on the seat.

"You're a good boy," she said.

I fought the urge to tell her, I'm not one of them. I'm not his son. I'm just the boy who lives next door, part-time. I'm no one, nothing. Instead I said, "I hope you feel better soon," and walked back toward the house.

Henry came out and on the ground where the lady's car had been, there was a photo, it must have fallen out of her purse, my hands, the car. It must have just slipped away and landed face up next to an oil stain.

"That's him," Henry said, picking up the photo, wiping it against his shirt, rubbing the boy's face over his heart.

"We should give it back to her."

"No," Henry said. "He's mine."

One afternoon while Mrs., baby June, and Henry were somewhere else, I watched Mr. digging a shallow trough through the yard. He was bent over a shovel, flipping clods of grass and dirt off to the side. He pulled a wilted piece of notebook paper from the back pocket of his shorts and consulted a diagram. Then, with his fingers as rulers, his feet as yardsticks, he began measuring his work. By the time I got from my bedroom window, across the tumor-o'-land, and into the Henrys' backyard, Mr. was sprinkling the floor of the trough with lima beans.

"What are you doing?" I asked as he opened a third bag of beans and dropped them one at a time into the trough. He didn't answer. "Planting?"

As soon as the beans were gone, he hauled over two large bags of charcoal briquettes and started laying the charcoal out over the beans.

"It looks like something out of *Gourmet* magazine," I said. "A new kind of barbecue recipe."

When he finished laying out all the charcoal, he sat down on a deck chair, took off his shoes and socks, pulled his shirt over his head, wiped his face and chest, dropped it down in a ball, and sighed a big one.

"They're not home yet?" he asked.

"Not yet," I said.

Mr. got up off the deck chair, picked up a can of starter fluid and went down the length of the trough, holding the can at crotch level, squeezing it so the fluid arced up like piss then softly splashed down onto the coals. In seconds the coals went from matte black to shiny wet and then back to matte black, as the stuff soaked in. He put down the can and picked up a box of those long fireplace matches.

"What's this supposed to be?" I asked. I thought it was probably another one of those things some people did that I just didn't know anything about.

Mr. Henry stood at the end of his trough, his runway of coal, lit three matches at once, held them in a tight fist, bowed his head, then dropped them in one by one. A line of flame spread the length of the ditch, sometimes golden, sometimes blue, sometimes spitting on itself. The coals shifted. Mr. stood at the end of the line looking down at his feet. He stepped out off the grass into the fire. In a split second he had both feet in the fire and was doing his best not to run. You could see it in his legs, in the muscles twitching.

"Don't," I shouted, going toward him.

He put both arms up in front of him, like someone sleepwalking, and the fluid that had splashed back on his hands ignited and his hands turned into ten fingers of flame, like a special effect, like something that would happen to a cartoon character. I stepped back and watched the flames jump three feet high, the hair on his arms and legs melt away, the edges of his shorts turn black, the flames at first just kissing him then starting to eat him alive. Mr. was silent until halfway down when he began to howl, to cry, and wail.

Mrs. came flying out the kitchen door, her purse over her arm, bag of groceries still in hand, screaming, "Don't just stand there, do something." She dropped the groceries and charged toward Mr. I ran into the Henrys' house and called the fire department. From the kitchen window, I could see Mrs. chasing Mr. around the yard, tackling him at the edge of the woods. The fire had reached out of the trough, chewed through the empty briquette bags, and was gnawing on the porch. I saw Henry and baby June standing off to the side, watching their mother in her Bermuda shorts lying on top of their father.

I went to the front door and waited for help.

Two days later, while Mr., all red and black, charred, swollen, bandaged, blotchy, with his arms and legs tied down, was still in intensive care, two men came and took away the remains of the new deck.

"He wants to be punished," Mrs. told the men. "Even though this was an accident, he's convinced it was his fault."

When they were gone Mrs. took the garden hose, a ladder, her trusty Playtex gloves and scrub brush, and with an industrial-sized bottle of lemon-lime Palmolive she washed the side of the house, the patio, and even the grass. "Go on down to the basement and bring up the beach things," she told Henry and me when she finished. "We're taking a few days off."

Henry and I plunged into the clammy cool of the basement, into the history packed away on deep wooden shelves Mr. had put up a few summers before. We took out all of Henry's old toys, played with them again, and lived our lives over. We did the memory quiz—do you remember when?—testing to see if we agreed on history, making sure we'd gotten everything right. We pulled out the beach chairs, inflatable rafts, and the Styrofoam cooler, and loaded them all into the back of Mrs.'s station wagon.

While Mrs. and baby June stayed at the foamy edge of the ocean, Henry and I danced in the waves, hurling ourselves toward them, daring the ocean to knock us out, to carry us away.

Despite our being coated with layers and layers of thick white sunblock, by the time the lifeguard pulled his station far back on the sand and walked off with the life preserver, we were red-hot like steamed lobsters.

We walked back to the motel dragging the beach chairs, the Styrofoam cooler, and all the extra sand our bathing suits would hold. To save time and hot water, Henry and I showered together and then turned the bathroom over to Mrs. and baby June. On our way out of the bathroom, Mrs. grabbed Henry by the head and recombed his hair the normal Henry way. He didn't stop her. He didn't rearrange it Stanton style.

Scrubbed and desalted, we sat at the four stations of the dinette set, eating two large and wonderful pizzas, drinking orange soda from cans, and simultaneously watching television. After dinner we all walked down the boardwalk watching seagulls plucking free food out of the sand and the sky and disappearing into darkness. Mrs. bought each of us a warm puffy ball of fried dough dipped in powdered sugar, and as we walked, baby June fell asleep in her mother's arms.

It was eight-thirty when we got back to the room. Mrs. lay down on the bed with baby June. Henry and I writhed around, pillow fighting, changing TV channels, and generally spinning on the edge until finally Mrs. had enough, took a twenty-dollar bill out of the nightstand, and told us to put on sweatshirts and long pants, to go out, and blow off some steam. "Be careful and have fun."

We raced out of the motel and back onto the boardwalk. Immediately, Henry bought a bucket of french fries and a Coke. We ate our way down the wooden planks, stopping to play darts and balloons, frog flip, and Skee-Ball, stuffing our pockets with cheap plush prizes. We bought vanilla-and-chocolate soft-swirl ice-cream cones, and fresh-made caramel corn. We sat on a bench eating while a summer's night parade of all human possibility swept by: deformed people, big families, small families, orphans, kids on first dates, guys in sawed-off leather jackets, old people. My skin was so hot from the sunburn that it felt cold. Shivery goose bumps covered my arms, legs, and the back of my neck. I was sugar-intoxicated. Music came out of every store, arcade, and refreshment stand, a thousand radios all tuned to a different station.

As we got closer to the amusement park at the end of the boardwalk, the music got louder, each little radio competing with the next, and all of them competing with the mechanical *oom pah pah* of the giant carousel that cut through the night. At the gates where the boardwalk met the park, everything melted into a multicolored, multiflavored, sensomatic, dizzying, swirly whirl. We had to run one way or the other, but couldn't stay there in the black hole of sensation. We charged toward the amusement park, toward the ticket booth. Henry slammed down what was left of the twenty and got two fist-fuls of tickets. We ran from ride to ride watching each one for a few seconds, deciding which were the best investments: Roller Coaster, Haunted House, Swiss Avalanche.

"That one definitely," Henry said, pointing across the park to spaceships taking off into the sky, trailing red-and-white afterglow. "Come on." We ran to the far edge of the park, to this last ride, sandwiched in the corner that touched the ocean. Rockets Round the Moon. There was a plot of grass, a metal chain-link fence and then barnacle-covered rocks, rail-road tie shoring, and the water evenly slapping against the edge of the world.

Henry gave the man our tickets and we slid past him and ran toward the space octopus, climbing into our own per-sonal rocket ship, pulling the chrome safety bar down in front of us. We took off smoothly, the giant mechanical arms swinging us high into the air, shifting, then throwing us out toward the sea, where we hung over the water for a second before being snapped back. We were pitching and swaying, more like a bucking bronco or something with transmission trouble than your typical flying machine. Henry threw him-self to the left and then to the right, slamming against me, getting the ship rocking in a rhythm all its own. The huge groaning arms flew us up, down, round and round. When we landed, Henry was absolutely sparkling. He pounded the side of our rocket, the hollow metal echoed. "Again, again," he shouted. The ride emptied and refilled. The ticket taker came by and Henry dropped too many tickets into his hand. The man counted them but didn't give any back. "More," Henry screamed. "More."

The ride started again and we were up, up, and away. Whirling, twirling. I closed my eyes and held on. I was being pulled in a thousand different directions. I was struggling to stay in one place. I could feel the force of being whipped through the air again and again starting to bend my face. I saw the picture from *Life* magazine of a man in a wind tunnel, his mouth stretched out, blown back, teeth and gums exposed. I was that man.

We landed smooth and safe, two feet above the ground. All there was to do was push the safety bar forward and step down and out.

"Once more, just once more," Henry said, digging into his pockets, dropping the last of the tickets into the man's hands.

We were airborne, we were flying, Rockets Round the Moon. I focused on the taillights of the ship in front of us, up and down, it went before us, side to side. Looking at it, I knew what would come next, I had a second to prepare. Up and away. Pushing off my knee, Henry stood. He rose up, steadied himself, then raised his arms up and open. His legs pressed against the safety bar. All of his weight was there. I pulled back on the bar hoping it would hold. I pulled back hoping Henry wouldn't take flight, fall free, roll out over the nose and into the sea. He stood in a trance, face taut, hair blowing, arms extended, scarecrow of the universe. Then his face dissolved into a colorless puddle of flesh. His jaw fell open, raw sewage spilled out and was whipped into the wind behind us. I slid down under the safety bar, onto the floor. I wrapped my arms around his legs, pressed my cheek to his knee, and pulled down. I looked up to see Henry still standing, his face covered with his own chunky blue. From the floor I could smell the noxiousness of its mixture, hot and rich, like some hearty soup a grandmother would serve on a winter night.

When we landed, the ticket man came running over with a bucket I thought was for Henry, but instead he flipped the safety bar back, pulled us out, and dumped a bucketful of sudsy water into the belly of our ship. "You fool," he yelled at Henry, who was unsteady on his feet, searching his pockets for more ride tickets, wiping his mouth with the sleeve of his sweatshirt. "Go back where you belong. Go home."

PLEASE REMAIN CALM

I wish I were dead. I have tried to keep it a secret, but it leaks out: "I wish I were dead," I blurted to the woman who is now my wife, the first morning we woke up together, the sheets still hot, stinking of sex.

"Should I take it personally?" she asked, covering herself.

"No," I said and began to cry.

"It's not so easy to die," she says. And she should know, she's a woman whose milieu is disaster—a specialist in emergency medicine. All day she is at work, putting the pieces back together and then she comes home to me. She tells me about the man run over by a train, how they carried in each of his legs in separate canvas bags. She tells me about the little boy doused in oil and deep-fried.

"Hi honey, I'm home," she says.

I hold my breath.

"I know you're here, your briefcase is in the front hall. Where are you?"

I wait to answer.

"Honey?"

I am sitting at the kitchen table.

"Today's the day," I tell her.

"What's different today?" she asks.

"Nothing. Nothing is different about today—that's the point. I feel the same today as I did yesterday and the day before. It's insufferable. Today," I repeat.

"Not today," she says.

"Now's the time," I say.

"Not the time."

"The moment has come."

"The moment has passed."

Every day I wish I didn't have to live a minute more, I wish I were someplace else, someplace new, someplace that never existed before. Death is a place without history, it's not like people have been there and then come back to tell you what a great time they had, that they highly recommend it, the food is wonderful and there's an incredible hotel right on the water.

"You think death is like Bali," my wife says.

We have been married for almost two years; she doesn't believe me anymore. It is as if I've cried wolf, screamed wolf, been a wolf, too many times.

"Did you stop at the store?"

I nod. I am in charge of the perishables, the things that must be consumed immediately. Every day on my way home I shop. Before I was married I would buy only one of each thing, a bottle of beer, a can of soup, a single roll of toilet paper—that sounds fine on a Monday when you think there will be no Tuesday, but what about late on Friday night when the corner store is closed?

My wife buys in bulk, she is forever stocking up, she is prepared in perpetuity.

"Did you remember milk?"

"I bought a quart."

"Not a half gallon?"

"You're lucky it's not a pint."

We are vigilant people, equally determined. The ongoing potential for things to go wrong is our bond—a fascination with crisis, with control. She likes to prevent, to repair, and I to wallow, to roll obsessively in the possibilities like some perverted pig. Our closets are packed with emergency supplies: freeze-dried food, a back-up generator, his and hers cans of Mace.

She opens a beer and flips through a catalog for emergency management specialists. This is how she relaxes— "What about gas masks? What if something happens, what if there's an event?"

I open a beer, take a breath. "I can't stand it anymore."

"You're stronger than you think."

I have spent nights laid low near the exhaust pipe of a car, have slept with a plastic bag over my head and silver duct tape around my neck. I have rifled through the kitchen drawers at three A.M. thinking I will have at myself with a carving knife. Once fresh from the shower, I divided myself in half, a clean incision from sternum to pubis. In the bathroom mirror, I watched what was leaking out of me, escaping me, with peculiar pleasure, not unlike the perverse pleasantry of taking a good shit. I arrived at the office dotted with the seeping red of my efforts. "Looks like you got a little on you," my secretary said, donating her seltzer to blot the spot. "You're always having these shaving accidents. Maybe you're cutting it too close."

All of the above is only a warm-up, a temporizing measure, a palliative remedy, I want something more, the big bang. If I had a gun I would use it, again and again, a million times a day I would shoot myself.

"What do you want to do about dinner?"

"Nothing. I never want to eat again."

"Not even steak?" my wife asks. "I was thinking I'd make us a nice thick steak. Yesterday you said, 'How come we never have steak anymore?' I took one out of the deep freeze this morning."

"Don't try to talk me out of it."

"Fine, but I'm having steak. Let me know if you change your mind."

There is a coldness to her, a chill I find terrifying, an

absence of emotion that puts a space between us, a permanent and unbridgeable gap—I am entirely emotion, she is entirely reason.

I will not change my mind. This isn't something new, something that started late in life. I've been this way since I was a child. It is the most awful addiction—the opposite of being a vampire and living off the blood of others, "eripmav"—sucked backward through life, the life cycle run in reverse, beginning in death and ending in . . .

Short of blowing my brains out, there is no way I can demonstrate the intensity, the extremity of my feeling. Click. Boom. Splat. The pain is searing, excruciating; the roots of my brain are hot with it.

"You can't imagine the pain I'm in."

"Take some Tylenol."

"Do you want me to make a salad?"

I have been married before, did I mention that? It ended badly—I ran into my ex-wife last week on the street and the color drained from both our faces; we're still weak from memory. "Are you all right?" I asked.

"I'm better," she said. "Much better. Alone." She quickly walked away.

There is an enormous amount of tension in being with someone who is dying every day. It's a perpetual hospice; the grief is too extreme. That's my specialty, pushing the limits, constantly testing people. No one can pass—that is the point. In the end, they crack, they leave, and I blame them.

I'm chopping lettuce.

"Caesar," my wife says, and I look up. She hands me a tin of anchovies. "Use the romaine."

"How was work?" There is relief in other people's tragedies.

"Interesting," she says, pulling the meat out of the broiler. She slices open the steak, blood runs out.

"How does that look?"

"Perfect." I smile, grating the Parmesan.

"A guy came in this afternoon, high on something. He'd tried to take his face off, literally—took a knife and peeled it."

"How did you put him back together?"

"A thousand stitches and surgical glue. Another man lost his right hand. Fortunately, he's a lefty."

We sit at the kitchen table talking about severed limbs, thin threads of ligaments, the delicate weave of nerves—reattachment, the hope of regaining full function. Miracles.

"I love you," she says, leaning over, kissing my forehead.

"How can you say that?"

"Because I do?"

"You don't love me enough."

"Nothing is enough," she says. And it is true, excruciatingly true.

I want to tell her I am having an affair, I want to make her leave, I want to prove that she doesn't love me enough. I want to have it over with.

"I'm having an affair," I tell her.

"No, you're not."

"Yes, I am. I'm fucking Sally Baumgarten."

She laughs. "And I'm giving blowjobs to Tom."

"My friend Tom?"

"You bet."

She could be, she very well could be. I pour Cascade into the dishwasher and push the button—Heavy Soil.

"I'm leaving," I tell her.

"Where are you going?"

"I don't know."

"When will you be back?"

"Never. I'm not coming back."

"Then you're not leaving," she says.

"I hate you."

I married her before I loved her. For our honeymoon, we went to California. She was thinking Disneyland, Carmel,

Big Sur, a driving trip up the coast—fun. I was hoping for an earthquake, brush fire, mudslide—disaster.

In the hotel room in Los Angeles I panicked. A wall of glass, a broad expanse of windows looking out over the city—it was a surprisingly clear night. The lights in the hills twinkled, beckoned. Without warning, I ran toward the glass, hurling myself forward.

She took me down, tackling me. She sat on top, pinning me, her one hundred nineteen pounds on my one fifty-six— she's stronger than you think.

"If you do that again I won't forgive you."

The intimacy, the unbearable intimacy is what's most mortifying—when they know the habits of your bowels, your cheapnesses, your horribleness, when they know things about you that no one should know, things you don't even know about yourself.

She knows these things and doesn't say it's too much, too weird, too fucked up. "It's my training," she says. "My shift doesn't end just because something bad happens."

It is about love. It is about getting enough, having enough, drowning in it, and now it is too late. I am permanently malnourished—there isn't enough love in the world.

There is a danger in this, in writing this, in saying this. I am putting myself on the line. If I am found floating, face down, there will be theories, lingering questions. Did he mean it? Was it an accident—is there any such thing as an accident, is fate that forgiving? Was this letter a warning, a true story? Everything is suspect. (Unless otherwise instructed—if something happens, give me the benefit of the doubt.)

"What would it be like if you gave it up?" she asked.

I am incredulous.

"If you abandoned the idea? Aren't you bored by it all after all these years; why not just give it up?"

"Wanting to be dead is as natural to me as breathing."

What would I be without it? I don't know that I could

handle it. Like being sprung from a lifetime jail, like Jack Henry Abbot, I might wheel around and stab someone with a dinner knife.

And what if I truly gave it up, if I said, yes it is a beautiful day, yes I am incredibly lucky—one of the luckiest men in the world. What if I admitted it, you are my best friend, my favorite fuck, my cure. What if I say I love you and she says it's over. What if that's part of the game, the dance? I will have missed my moment, I will be shit out of luck—stuck here forever.

"Why do you put up with it?"

"Because this is not you," she says. "It's part of you, but it's not you. Are you still going to kill yourself?"

"Yes," I say. Yes I am, to prove I am independent, to prove I still can. "I hate you," I tell her. "I hate you so much."

"I know," she says.

My wife is not without complications of her own. She keeps a baseball bat under her side of the bed. I discovered it by accident—one day it rolled out from under. Louisville Slugger. I rolled it back into place and have never let on that I know it's there. Sometimes she wakes up in the middle of the night, sits straight up, and screams, "Who's there? Who is in the waiting room?" She stops for a second and starts again, annoyed. "I don't have all day. Next. Bring the next one in." There are nights I watch her sleep, her face a naive dissolve, tension erased, her delicate blond lashes, her lips, soft like a child's, and I want to punch her. I want to bash her face in. I wonder what she would do then.

"A thought is only a thought," she says when I wake her.

And then she tells me her dreams. "I was a man and I was having sex with another man and you were there, you were wearing a white skirt, and then someone came in but he didn't have any arms and I kept wondering how did he open the door?"

"Let's go back to sleep for a little while."

I am getting closer. The situation is untenable, something has to happen. I have lived this way for a long time, there is a cumulative effect, a worsening. I am embarrassed that I have let it go on for so long.

I know how I will do it. I will hang myself. Right here at home. I have known it since we bought the house. When the real estate agent went on and on about the location, the yard, the school district, I was thinking about the interior—the exposed rafters, the beams. The dead man's walk to the top of the stairs.

We are cleaning up. I wipe the table with a sponge.

"What's in the bag," she says, pointing to something on the counter.

"Rope." I stopped on the way home. I ran the errand.

"Let's go to the movies," she says, tying up the trash. She hands me the bag. "Take it outside," she says, sending me into the night.

The yard is flooded with light, extra lights, like search-lights, lights so bright that when raccoons cross to get to the trash, they hold their paws up over their eyes, shielding them.

I feel her watching me from the kitchen window.

We go to see *The Armageddon Complex,* a disaster film with a tidal wave, a tornado, a fire, a global-warming theme. Among the special effects are that the temperature in the theater changes from 55 to 90 degrees during the film—*You freeze, you cook, you wish you'd planned ahead.*

The popcorn is oversalted. Before the tidal wave hits, I am panting with thirst. "Water," I whisper, climbing over her into the aisle.

She pulls me back into my seat. "Don't go."

At key moments, she covers her eyes and waits until I squeeze her free hand to give her the all clear.

We are in the car on the way home. She is driving. The night is black. We move through the depths of darkness—the thin yellow line, the pathway home, unfolds before us. There is the hum of the engine, the steadiness of her foot on the gas.

"We have to talk," I tell her.

"We talk constantly. We never stop talking."

"There's something I need to . . ." I say, not finishing the thought.

A deer crosses the road. My wife swerves. The car goes up a hill, trees fly by, the car goes down, we are rolling, we are hanging upside-down, suspended, and then boom, we are upright again, the air bag smashes me in the face, punches me in the nose. The steering wheel explodes into her chest. We are down in a ditch with balloons pressed into our faces, suffocating.

"Are you hurt?" she asks.

"I'm fine," I say. "Are you all right?"

"Did we hit it?"

"No, I think it got away."

The doors unlock.

"I'm sorry," she says, "I'm so sorry. I didn't see it coming."

The air bags are slowly deflating—losing pressure.

"I want to live," I tell her. "I just don't know how."

THINGS YOU SHOULD KNOW

There are things I do not know. I was absent the day they passed out the information sheets. I was home in bed with a fever and an earache. I lay with the heating pad pressed to my head, burning my ear. I lay with the heating pad until my mother came in and said, "Don't keep it on high or you'll burn yourself." This was something I knew but chose to forget.

The information sheets had the words "Things You Should Know" typed across the top of the page. They were mimeographed pages, purple ink on white paper. The sheets were written by my fourth grade teacher. They were written when she was young and thought about things. She thought of a language for these things and wrote them down in red Magic Marker.

By the time she was my teacher, she'd been teaching for a very long time but had never gotten past fourth grade. She hadn't done anything since her Things You Should Know sheets, which didn't really count, since she'd written them while she was still a student.

After my ear got better, the infection cured, the red burn mark faded into a sort of a Florida tan, I went back to school. Right away I knew I'd missed something important. "Ask the other students to fill you in on what happened while you were ill," the principal said when I handed her the note from my mother. But none of the others would talk to me. Immediately I knew this was because they'd gotten the information sheets and we no longer spoke the same language.

I tried asking the teacher, "Is there anything I missed while I was out?" She handed me a stack of maps to color in and some math problems. "You should put a little Vaseline on your ear," she said. "It'll keep it from peeling."

"Is there anything else?" I asked. She shook her head.

I couldn't just come out and say it. I couldn't say, you know, those information sheets, the ones you passed out the other day while I was home burning my ear. Do you have an extra copy? I couldn't ask because I'd already asked everyone. I asked so many people—my parents, their friends, random strangers—that in the end they sent me to a psychiatrist.

"What exactly do you think is written on this 'Things to Know' paper?" he asked me.

"'Things You Should Know,'" I said. "It's not things to know, not things you will learn, but things you already should know but maybe are a little dumb, so you don't."

"Yes," he said, nodding. "And what are those things?"

"You're asking me," I shouted. "I don't know. You're the one who should know. You tell me. I never saw the list."

Time passed. I grew up. I grew older. I grew deaf in one ear. In the newspaper I read that the teacher had died. She was eighty-four. In time I began to notice there was less to know. All the same, I kept looking for the list. Once, in an old bookstore, I thought I found page four. It was old, faded, folded into quarters and stuffed into an early volume of Henry Miller's essays. The top part of the page had been torn off. It began with number six: "Do what you will because you will anyway." Number twenty-eight was "If you begin and it is not the beginning, begin again." And so on. At the bottom of the page it said, "Chin San Fortune Company lines 1 through 32."

Years later, when I was even older, when those younger than me seemed to know less than I ever had, I wrote a story. And in a room full of people, full of people who knew the list and some I was sure did not, I stood to read. "As a child, I burned my ear into a Florida tan."

"Stop," a man yelled, waving his hands at me.

"Why?"

"Don't you know?" he said. I shook my head. He was a man who knew the list, who probably had his own personal copy. He had based his life on it, on trying to explain it to others.

He spoke, he drew diagrams, splintering poles of chalk as he put pictures on a blackboard. He tried to tell of the things he knew. He tried to talk but did not have the language of the teacher.

I breathed deeply and thought of Chin San number twenty-eight. "If you begin and it is not the beginning, begin again."

"I will begin again," I announced. Because I had stated this and had not asked for a second chance, because I was standing and he was seated, because it was still early in the evening, the man who had stopped me nodded, all right.

"Things You Should Know," I said.

"Good title, good title," the man said. "Go on, go on."

"There is a list," I said, nearing the end. "It is a list you make yourself. And at the top of the page you write, 'Things You Should Know.'"

THE WHIZ KIDS

In the big bathtub in my parents' bedroom, he ran his tongue along my side, up into my armpits, tugging the hair with his teeth. "We're like married," he said, licking my nipples.

I spit at him. A foamy blob landed on his bare chest. He smiled, grabbed both my arms, and held them down.

He slid his face down my stomach, dipped it under the water, and put his mouth over my cock.

My mother knocked on the bathroom door. "I have to get ready. Your father and I are leaving in twenty minutes."

Air bubbles crept up to the surface.

"Can you hear me?" she said, fiddling with the knob. "Why is the door locked? You know we don't lock doors in this house."

"It was an accident," I said through the door.

"Well, hurry," my mother said.

And we did.

Later, in the den, picking his nose, examining the results on his finger, slipping his finger into his mouth with a smack and a pop, he explained that as long as we never slept with anyone else, we could do whatever we wanted. "Sex kills," he said, "but this," he said, "this is the one time, the only time, the chance of a lifetime." He ground his front teeth on the booger.

We met in a science class. "Cocksucker," he hissed. My fingers were in my ears. I didn't hear the word so much as saw it escape his mouth. The fire alarm was going off. Everyone was grabbing their coats and hurrying for the door. He held me back, pressed his lips close to my ear, and said it again, Cocksucker, his tongue touching my neck. Back and forth, he shook a beaker of a strange potion and threatened to make me drink it. He raised the glass to my mouth. My jaws clamped shut. With his free hand, he pinched my nostrils shut and laughed like a maniac. My mouth fell open. He tilted the beaker toward my throat. The teacher stopped him just in time. "Enough horsing around," she said. "This is a fire drill. Behave accordingly."

"Got ya," he said, pushing me into the hall and toward the steps, his hard-on rubbing against me the whole way down.

My mother came in, stood in front of the television set, her ass in Peter Jennings's face, and asked, "How do I look?"

He curled his lip and spit a pistachio shell onto the coffee table.

"Remember to clean up," my mother said.

"I want you to fuck me," he said while my father was in the next room, looking for his keys.

"Have you seen them?" my father asked.

"No," I said.

"I want your Oscar Mayer in my bun," he said.

He lived miles away, had gone to a different elementary school, was a different religion, wasn't circumcised.

My father poked his head into the room, jiggled his keys in the air, and said, "Got 'em."

"Great tie," I said.

My father tweaked his bow tie. "Bye, guys."

The front door closed. My father's white Chrysler slid into the street.

"I want you to give it to me good."

"I want to watch *Jeopardy,*" I said, going for the remote control.

"Ever tasted a dick infusion?" he asked, sipping from my glass of Dr. Pepper.

He unzipped his fly, fished out his dick, and dropped it into the glass. The ice cubes melted, cracking the way they do when you pour in something hot. A minute later, he put his dick away, swirled the soda around, and offered me a sip.

"Maybe later," I said, focusing on the audio daily double. " 'Tie a Yellow Ribbon.' "

"I'm bored," he said.

"Play along," I said. "I've already got nine thousand dollars."

He went to the bookcase and started handling the family photos. "Wonder if he ever sucked a cock," he said, picking up a portrait of my father.

"Don't be a butt plug."

He smiled. "I love you," he said, raising his T-shirt, pulling it off over his head.

Dark hair rose in a fishbone up and out of his jeans.

I turned off the television.

"We need something," he said as I led him down the hall toward my room.

"Something what?"

"Slippery."

I ducked into the bathroom, opened the cabinet, and grabbed a tube of Neosporin.

"Brilliant," he said. "An antibiotic lube job, fights infection while you're having fun."

Piece by piece I undressed with him, after him. He peeled off his socks, I peeled off mine. He unzipped his jeans and I undid mine. He slipped his fingers into the band of his underwear, snapped the elastic, and grinned. I pulled mine down. He slipped the tube of ointment into my ass, pinched my nipples, and sank his teeth deep into the muscle above my collarbone.

My parents got back just after midnight. "It was so nice of you to spend the evening," my mother said. "I just hate to leave you-know-who home alone. I think he gets depressed."

"Whatever," he said, shrugging. He left with my father, who was giving him a ride home.

"You don't have to come with us," my father said to me. "It's late. Go to bed."

"See you in school tomorrow," I said.

"Whatever."

A week later he sat in my room at home, jerking off, with the door open.

"Stop," I said. "Or close the door."

"Danger excites me."

"My mother isn't dangerous," I said, getting up and closing the door myself.

"What we've got here," he said, still jerking, "is virgin sperm. People will pay a load for this shit." He laughed at himself. "Get it—pay a load." Come shot into the air and landed on the glass of my fish tank.

"Very funny," I said. I was working out an algebra problem on my bed. He came over to me, dropped his pants, and put his butt in my face. "Your luck, I haven't used it for anything except a couple of farts all day. Lick it," he said, bending over, holding his cheeks apart. It was smelly and permanently stained. His testicles hung loose and low, and I took them in my hand, rolling them like Bogart's *Caine Mutiny* balls. "Get in," he said. I buried my face there, tickled his asshole with the tip of my tongue, and made him laugh.

Saturday, on her way to the grocery store, my mother dropped us off at the park. "Shall I come back for you when I'm finished?" she asked.

"No," he said flatly.

"No, thanks," I said. "We'll find our way."

"Ever fuck a girl?" he asked as we cut across the grass, past the playground, past the baseball fields and toward the woods.

"No."

"Ever want to?"

"No."

"Wanna watch?" he said, taking me to a picnic table where a girl I recognized from school was standing, arms crossed in front of her chest. "It's twelve-thirty, you're late," she said. The girl looked at me and blinked. "Oh, hi. We're in history together, right?"

I nodded and looked at my shoes.

"Miss me?" he asked, kissing the girl's neck, hard.

My eyes hyperfocused and zeroed in on his lips, on her skin, on the feathery blond hair at the base of her skull. When he pulled away, the hair was wet, the skin was purple and red. There were teeth marks.

She stood in the clearing, eyes closed. He reached for her hand and led her into the woods. I followed, keeping a certain distance between them and me.

In the trees, he pulled his T-shirt off over his head. She ran her fingernails slowly up and down the fishbone of fur sticking out of his Levi's. He tugged at the top of her jeans.

"Take 'em off," he said in a familiar and desperate voice.

"Who do you think you're kidding," she said.

"Show me yours," he said, rubbing the front of his Levi's with an open palm, "and I'll show you mine."

"That's okay, thanks," she said, backing away.

He went toward her, she stepped back again. He stuck his leg behind her, tripping her. She fell to the ground. He stepped on her open palms, holding her down with his Nikes.

"This isn't funny," she said.

He laughed.

He unzipped his pants and peed on her. She screamed, and he aimed the river at her mouth. Her lips sealed and her head turned away. Torrent released, he shook it off on her, put it away, and stepped from her hands.

She raised herself. Urine ran down her cheeks, onto her blouse, and into her jeans. Arms spread, faces twisted, together she and I ran out of the woods, screaming as though doused in gasoline, as though afire.

DO NOT DISTURB

My wife, the doctor, is not well. In the end she could be dead. It started suddenly, on a country weekend, a movie with friends, a pizza, and then pain. "I liked the part where he lunged at the woman with a knife," Eric says.

"She deserved it," Enid says.

"Excuse me," my wife says, getting up from the table.

A few minutes later I find her doubled over on the sidewalk. "Something is ripping me from the inside out."

"Should I get the check?" She looks at me like I am an idiot.

"My wife is not well," I announce, returning to the table. "We have to go."

"What do you mean—is she all right?"

Eric and Enid hurry out while I wait for the check. They drive us home. As I open the front door, my wife pushes past me and goes running for the bathroom. Eric, Enid, and I stand in the living room, waiting.

"Are you all right in there?" I call out.

"No," she says.

"Maybe she should go to the hospital," Enid says.

"Doctors don't go to the hospital," I say.

She lies on the bathroom floor, her cheek against the white tile. "I keep thinking it will pass."

"Call us if you need us," Eric and Enid say, leaving.

I tuck the bath mat under her head and sneak away. From the kitchen I call a doctor friend. I stand in the dark, whispering, "She's just lying there on the floor, what do I do?"

"Don't do anything," the doctor says, half-insulted by the thought that there is something to do. "Observe her. Either it will go away, or something more will happen. You watch and you wait."

Watch and wait. I am thinking about our relationship. We haven't been getting along. The situation has become oxygenless and addictive, a suffocating annihilation, each staying to see how far it will go.

I sit on the edge of the tub, looking at her. "I'm worried."

"Don't worry," she says. "And don't just sit there staring."

Earlier in the afternoon we were fighting, I don't remember about what. I only know—I called her a bitch.

"I was a bitch before I met you and I'll be a bitch long after you're gone. Surprise me," she said. "Tell me something new."

I wanted to say, I'm leaving. I wanted to say, I know you think I never will and that's why you treat me like you do. But I'm going. I wanted to get in the car, drive off, and call it a day.

The fight ended with the clock. She glanced at it. "It's six-thirty, we're meeting Eric and Enid at seven; put on a clean shirt."

She is lying on the bathroom floor, the print of the bath mat making an impression on her cheek. "Are you comfortable?" I ask.

She looks surprised, as though she's just realized she's on the floor.

"Help me," she says, struggling to get up.

Her lips are white and thin.

"Bring me a trash can, a plastic bag, a thermometer, some Tylenol, and a glass of water."

"Are you going to throw up?"

"I want to be prepared," she says.

We are always prepared. We have flare guns and fire extinguishers, walkie talkies, a rubber raft, a hundred batteries in assorted shapes and sizes, a thousand bucks in dollar bills, enough toilet paper and bottled water to get us through six months. When we travel we have smoke hoods in our carry-on bags, protein bars, water purification tablets, and a king-sized bag of M&Ms. We are ready and waiting.

She slips the digital thermometer under her tongue; the numbers move up the scale—each beep is a tenth of a degree.

"A hundred and one point four," I announce.

"I have a fever?" she says in disbelief.

"I wish things between us weren't so bad."

"It's not as bad as you think," she says. "Expect less and you won't be disappointed."

We try to sleep; she is hot, she is cold, she is mumbling something about having "a surgical belly," something about "guarding and rebound." I don't know if she's talking about herself or the NBA.

"This is incredible." She sits bolt upright and folds over again, writhing. "Something is struggling inside me. It's like one of those alien movies, like I'm going to burst open and something's going to spew out, like I'm erupting." She pauses, takes a breath. "And then it stops. Who would ever have thought this would happen to me—and on a Saturday night?"

"Is it your appendix?"

"That's the one thought I have, but I'm not sure. I don't have the classic symptoms. I don't have anorexia or diarrhea. When I was eating that pizza, I was hungry."

"Is it an ovary? Women have lots of ovaries."

"Women have two ovaries," she says. "It did occur to me that it could be Mittelschmertz."

"Mittelschmertz?"

"The launching of the egg, the middle of the cycle."

At five in the morning her temperature is one hundred and three. She is alternately sweating and shivering.

"Should I drive you back to the city or to the hospital out here?"

"I don't want to be the doctor who goes to the ER with gas."

"Fine."

I am dressing myself, packing, thinking of what I will need in the waiting room: cell phone, notebook, pen, something to read, something to eat, my wallet, her insurance card.

We are in the car, hurrying. There is an urgency to the situation, the unmistakable sense that something bad is happening. I am driving seventy miles an hour.

She is not a doctor now. She is lost, inside herself.

"I think I'm dying," she says.

I pull up to the emergency entrance and half-carry her in, leaving the car doors open, the engine running; I have the impulse to drop her off and walk away.

The emergency room is empty. There is a bell on the check-in desk. I ring it twice.

A woman appears. "Can I help you?"

"My wife is not well," I say. "She is a doctor."

The woman sits at her computer. She takes my wife's name. She takes her insurance card and then she takes her temperature and blood pressure. "Are you in a lot of pain?"

"Yes," my wife says.

Within minutes a doctor is there, pressing on my wife. "It's got to come out," he says.

"What?" I ask.

"Appendix. Do you want some Demerol?"

She shakes her head. "I'm working tomorrow and I'm on call."

In the cubicle next to her, someone vomits.

The nurse comes to take blood. "They called Barry Manilow—he's a very good surgeon." She ties off my wife's arm. "We call him Barry Manilow because he looks like Barry Manilow."

"I want to do right by you," Barry Manilow says, as he's

feeling my wife's belly. "I'm not sure it's your appendix, not sure it's your gall bladder either. I'm going to call the radiologist and let him scan it. How's that sound?" She nods.

I take the surgeon aside. "Should she be staying here? Is this the place to do this?"

"It's not a kidney transplant," he says.

The nurse brings me a cold drink. She offers me a chair. I sit close to the gurney where my wife lies. "Do you want me to get you out of here? I could hire a car and have us driven to the city. I could have you medevaced home."

"I don't want to go anywhere," she says. She is on the wrong side of it now.

Back in the cubicle, Barry Manilow is talking to her. "It's not your appendix. It's your ovary. It's a hemmorhagic cyst; you're bleeding and your hematocrit is falling. We have to operate. I've called a gynecologist and the anesthesiologist—I'm just waiting for them to arrive. We're going to take you upstairs very soon."

"Just do it," she says.

I stop Barry Manilow in the hall. "Can you try and save the ovary, she very much wants to have children. It's just something she hasn't gotten around to yet—first she had her career, then me, and now this."

"We'll do everything we can," he says, disappearing through the door marked "Authorized Personnel Only."

I am the only one in the surgical waiting room, flipping through copies of *Field and Stream, Highlights for Children*, a pamphlet on colon cancer. Less than an hour later, Barry Manilow comes to find me. "We saved the ovary. We took out something the size of a lemon."

"The size of a lemon?"

He makes a fist and holds it up—"A lemon," he says. "It looked a little funny. We sent it to Pathology." He shrugs.

A lemon, a bleeding lemon, like a blood orange, a lemon souring in her. Why is fruit used as the universal medical measurement?

"She should be upstairs in about an hour."

When I get to her room she is asleep. A tube poking out from under the covers drains urine into a bag. She is hooked up to oxygen and an IV.

I put my hand on her forehead. Her eyes open.

"A little fresh air," she says, pulling at the oxygen tube. "I always wondered what all this felt like."

She has a morphine drip, the kind she can control herself. She keeps the clicker in hand. She never pushes the button.

I feed her ice chips and climb into the bed next to her. In the middle of the night I go home. In the morning she calls, waking me up.

"Flowers have been arriving like crazy," she says, "from the hospital, from the ER, from the clinic."

Doctors are like firemen. When one of their own is down they go crazy.

"They took the catheter out, I'm sitting up in a chair. I already had some juice and took myself to the bathroom," she says proudly. "They couldn't be nicer. But, of course, I'm a very good patient."

I interrupt her. "Do you want anything from the house?"

"Clean socks, a pair of sweat pants, my hairbrush, some toothpaste, my face soap, a radio, maybe a can of Diet Coke."

"You're only going to be there a couple of days."

"You asked if I needed anything. Don't forget to feed the dog."

Five minutes later she calls back, crying. "I have ovarian cancer."

I run out the door. When I get there the room is empty. I'm expecting a big romantic scene, expecting her to cling to me, to tell me how much she loves me, how she's sorry we've been having such a hard time, how much she needs me, wants me, now more than ever. The bed is empty. For a moment I think she's died, jumped out the window, escaped. Her absence is terrifying.

In the bathroom, the toilet flushes. "I want to go home," she says, stepping out, fully dressed.

"Do you want to take the flowers?"

"They're mine, aren't they? Do you think all the nurses know I have cancer? I don't want anyone to know."

The nurse comes with a wheelchair; she takes us down to the lobby. "Good luck," she says, loading the flowers into the car.

"She knows," my wife says.

We are on the Long Island Expressway. I am dialing and driving. I call my wife's doctor in New York.

"She has to see Kibbowitz immediately," the doctor says.

"Do you think I'll lose my ovary?"

She will lose everything—instinctively I know that.

We are home. She is on the bed with the dog on her lap. She peeks beneath the gauze; her incision is crooked, the lack of precision an incredible insult. "Do you think they can fix it?"

In the morning we go to Kibbowitz. She is again on a table, her feet in the stirrups, in launch position, waiting. Before the doctor arrives she is interviewed and examined by seven medical students. I hate them. I hate them for talking to her, for touching her, for wasting her time. I hate Kibbowitz for keeping her on the table for more than an hour, waiting.

And she is angry with me for being annoyed. "They're just doing their job."

Kibbowitz arrives. He is enormous, like a hockey player, a brute and a bully. It is hard to understand how a man gets gynecologic oncology as his calling. I can tell immediately that she likes him. She will do anything he says.

"Scootch down a little closer to me," he says, settling himself on a stool between her legs. She lifts her ass and slides down. He examines her. He looks under the gauze— "Crooked," he says. "Get dressed and meet me in my office."

"I want a number," she says. "A survival rate."

"I don't deal in numbers," he says.

"I need a number."

He shrugs. "How's seventy percent?"

"Seventy percent what?"

"Seventy percent live five years."

"And then what?" I ask.

"And then some don't," he says.

"What has to come out?" she asks.

"What do you want to keep?"

"I wanted to have a child."

This is a delicate negotiation; they talk parts. "I could take just the one ovary," he says. "And then after the chemo you could try and get pregnant and then after you had a child we could go in and get the rest."

"Can you really get pregnant after chemo?" I ask.

The doctor shrugs. "Miracles happen all the time," he says. "The problem is you can't raise a child if you're dead. You don't have to decide now, let me know in a day or two. Meanwhile I'll book the operating room for Friday morning. Nice meeting you," he says, shaking my hand.

"I want to have a baby," she says.

"I want to have you," I say.

Beyond that I say nothing. Whatever I say she will do the opposite. We are at that point—spite, blame, and fault. I don't want to be held responsible. She opens the door of the consulting room. "Doctor," she shouts, hurrying down the hall after him, clutching her belly, her incision, her wound. "Take it," she screams. "Take it all the hell out."

He is standing outside another examination room, chart in hand.

He nods. "We'll take it through your vagina. We'll take the ovaries, the uterus, cervix, omentum, and your appendix, if they didn't already get it in Southampton. And then we'll put a port in your chest and sign you up for chemotherapy—eight rounds should do it."

She nods.

"See you Friday."

We leave. I am holding her hand, holding her pocketbook on my shoulder, trying to be as good as anyone can be.

"Why don't they just say 'eviscerate'? Why don't they just come out and say, on Friday at nine we're going to eviscerate you—be ready."

"Do you want a little lunch? Some soup? There's a lovely restaurant near here."

She looks flushed. I put my hand to her forehead. She's burning up. "You have a fever. Did you mention that to the doctor?"

"It's not relevant."

Later, when we are home, I ask, "Do you remember our third date? Do you remember asking—how would you kill yourself if you had to do it with bare hands? I said I would break my nose and shove it up into my brain, and you said you would reach up with your bare hands and rip your uterus out through your vagina and throw it across the room."

"What's your point?"

"No point—I just suddenly remembered it. Isn't Kibbowitz taking your uterus out through your vagina?"

"I doubt he's going to throw it across the room," she says. There is a pause. "You don't have to stay with me now that I have cancer. I don't need you. I don't need anyone. I don't need anything."

"If I left, I wouldn't be leaving because you have cancer. But I would look like an ass, everyone would think I couldn't take it."

"I would make sure they knew it was me, that I was a monster, a cold steely monster, that I drove you away."

"They wouldn't believe you."

She suddenly farts and runs, embarrassed, into the bathroom—as though this is the first time she's farted in her life. "My life is ruined," she yells, slamming the door.

148

"Farting is the least of it."

When she comes out she is calmer, she crawls into bed next to me, wrung out, shivering.

I hold her. "Do you want to make love?"

"You mean one last time before I'm not a woman, before I'm a dried old husk?"

Instead of fucking we fight. It's the same sort of thing, dramatic, draining. When we're done, I roll over and sleep in a tight knot on my side of the bed.

"Surgical menopause," she says. "That sounds so final." I turn toward her. She runs her hand over her pubic hair. "Do you think they'll shave me?"

I am not going to be able to leave the woman with cancer. I am not the kind of person who leaves the woman with cancer, but I don't know what you do when the woman with cancer is a bitch. Do you hope that the cancer prompts the woman to reevaluate herself, to take it as an opportunity, a signal for change? As far as she's concerned there is no such thing as the mind-body connection; there is science and there is law. There is fact and everything else is bullshit.

Friday morning, while she is in the hospital registration area waiting for her number to be called, she makes another list out loud: "My will is in the top left drawer of the dresser. If anything goes wrong, pull the plug. No heroic measures. I want to be cremated. Donate my organs. Give it away, all of it, every last drop." She stops. "I guess no one will want me now that I'm contaminated." She says the word "contaminated" filled with disgust, disappointment, as though she has failed, soiled herself.

It is nearly eight P.M. when Kibbowitz comes out to tell me he's done. "Everything was stuck together like macaroni and cheese. It took longer than I expected. I found some in the fallopian tube and some on the wall of her abdomen. We cleaned everything out."

She is wheeled back to her room, sad, agitated, angry.

"Why didn't you come and see me?" she asks accusatorily.

"I was right there the whole time, on the other side of the door, waiting for word."

She acts as though she doesn't believe me, as though I screwed with a secretary from the patient services office while she was on the table.

"How're you feeling?"

"Like I've taken a trip to another country and my suitcases are lost."

She is writhing. I adjust her pillow, the position of the bed.

"What hurts?"

"What doesn't hurt? Everything hurts. Breathing hurts."

Because she is a doctor, because she did her residency at this hospital, they give me a small folding cot to set up in the corner of the room. Bending to unfold it, something happens in my back, a hot searing pain spreads across and down. I lower myself to the floor, grabbing the blanket as I go.

Luckily she is sleeping.

The nurse who comes to check her vital signs sees me. "Are you in trouble?"

"It's happened before," I say. "I'll just lie here and see where it goes."

She brings me a pillow and covers me with the blanket.

Eric and Enid arrive. My wife is asleep and I am still on the floor. Eric stands over me.

"We're sorry," Eric whispers. "We didn't get your message until today. We were at Enid's parents'—upstate."

"It's shocking, it's sudden, it's so out of the blue." Enid moves to look at my wife. "She looks like she's in a really bad mood, her brow is furrowed. Is she in pain?"

"I assume so."

"If there's anything we can do, let us know," Eric says.

"Actually, could you walk the dog?" I pull the keys out of my pocket and hold them in the air. "He's been home alone all day."

"Walk the dog—I think we can do that," Eric says, looking at Enid for confirmation.

"We'll check on you in the morning," Enid says.

"Before you go; there's a bottle of Percoset in her purse—give me two."

During the night she wakes up. "Where are you?" she asks.

"I'm right here."

She is sufficiently drugged that she doesn't ask for details. At around six she opens her eyes and sees me on the floor.

"Your back?"

"Yep."

"Cancer beats back," she says and falls back to sleep.

When the cleaning man comes with the damp mop, I pry myself off the floor. I'm fine as long as I'm standing.

"You're walking like you have a rod up your ass," my wife says.

"Is there anything I can do for you?" I ask, trying to be solicitous.

"Can you have cancer for me?"

The pain management team arrives to check on my wife's level of comfort.

"On a scale of one to ten, how do you feel?" the pain fellow asks.

"Five," my wife says.

"She lies," I say.

"Are you lying?"

"How can you tell?"

The specialist arrives. "I know you," he says, seeing my wife in the bed. "We went to school together."

My wife tries to smile.

"You were the smartest one in the class and now look," he reads my wife's chart. "Ovarian cancer and you, that's horrible."

*   *   *

My wife is sitting up high in her hospital bed, puking her guts into a metal bucket, like a poisoned pet monkey. She is throwing up bright green like an alien. Ted, her boss, stares at her, mesmerized.

The room is filled with people—people I don't know, medical people, people she went to school with, people she did her residency with, a man whose fingers she sewed back on, relatives I've not met. I don't understand why they don't excuse themselves, why they don't step out of the room. I don't understand why there is no privacy. They're all watching her like they've never seen anyone throw up before—riveted.

She is not sleeping. She is not eating. She is not getting up and walking around. She is afraid to leave her bed, afraid to leave her bucket.

I make a sign for the door. I borrow a black Magic Marker from the charge nurse and print in large black letters, DO NOT DISTURB.

They push the door open. They come bearing gifts, flowers, food, books. "I saw the sign, I assumed it was for someone else."

I am wiping green spittle from her lips.

"Do you want me to get rid of everyone?" I ask.

I want to get rid of everyone. The idea that these people have some claim to her, some right to entertain, distract, bother her more than I, drives me up the wall. "Should I tell them to go?"

She shakes her head. "Just the flowers, the flowers nauseate me."

An hour later, I empty the bucket again. The room remains overcrowded. I am on my knees by the side of her hospital bed, whispering, "I'm leaving."

"Are you coming back?" she whispers.

"No."

She looks at me strangely. "Where are you going?"

"Away."

"Bring me a Diet Coke."

She has missed the point.

It is heartbreaking seeing her in a stained gown, in the middle of a bed, unable to tell everyone to go home, unable to turn it off. Her pager is clipped to her hospital gown, several times it goes off. She returns the calls. She always returns the calls. I imagine her saying, "What the hell are you bothering me for—I'm busy, I'm having cancer."

Later, I am on the edge of the bed, looking at her. She is increasingly beautiful, more vulnerable, female.

"Honey?"

"What?" Her intonation is like a pissy caged bird—*cawww*. "What? What are you looking at? What do you want?" *Cawww*.

"Nothing."

I am washing her with a cool washcloth.

"You're tickling me," she complains.

"Make sure you tell her you still find her attractive," a man in the hall tells me. "Husbands of women who have mastectomies need to keep reminding their wives that they are beautiful."

"She had a hysterectomy," I say.

"Same thing."

Two days later, they remove the packing. I am in the room when the resident comes with a long tweezers like tongs and pulls yards of material from her vagina, wads of cotton, and gauze, stained battlefield red. It's like a magic trick gone awry, one of those jokes about how many people you can fit in a telephone booth, more and more keeps coming out.

"Is there anything left in there?" she asks.

The resident shakes his head. "Your vagina now just comes to a stop, it's a stump, an unconnected sleeve. Don't be surprised if you bleed, if you pop a stitch or two." He checks her chart and signs her out. "Kibbowitz has you on pelvic rest for six weeks."

"Pelvic rest?" I ask.

"No fucking," she says.

Not a problem.

Home. She watches forty-eight hours of Holocaust films on cable TV. Although she claims to compartmentalize everything, suddenly she identifies with the bald, starving prisoners of war. She sees herself as a victim. She points to the naked corpse of a woman. "That's me," she says. "That's exactly how I feel."

"She's dead," I say.

"Exactly."

Her notorious vigilance is gone. As I'm fluffing her pillows, her billy club rolls out from under the bed. "Put it in the closet," she says.

"Why?" I ask, rolling it back under the bed.

"Why sleep with a billy club under the bed? Why do anything when you have cancer?"

During a break between *Shoah* and *The Sorrow and the Pity*, she taps me. "I'm missing my parts," she says. "Maybe one of those lost eggs was someone special, someone who would have cured something, someone who would have invented something wonderful. You never know who was in there. They are my lost children."

"I'm sorry."

"For what?" she looks at me accusingly.

"Everything."

"Thirty-eight-year-olds don't get cancer, they get Lyme disease, maybe they have appendicitis, on rare occasions in some other parts of the world they have Siamese twins, but that's it."

In the middle of the night she wakes up, she throws the covers off. "I can't breathe, I'm burning up. Open the window, I'm hot, I'm so hot."

"Do you know what's happening to you?"

"What are you talking about?"

"You're having hot flashes."

"I am not," she says, as though I've insulted her. "They don't start so soon."

They do.

"Get away from me, get away," she yells. "Just being near you makes me uncomfortable, it makes my temperature unstable."

On Monday she starts chemotherapy.

"Will I go bald?" she asks the nurse.

I cannot imagine my wife bald.

"Most women buy a wig before it happens," the nurse says, plugging her into the magic potion.

One of the other women, her head wrapped in a red turban, leans over and whispers, "My husband says I look like a porno star." She winks. She has no eyebrows, no eyelashes, nothing.

We shop for a wig. She tries on every style, every shape and color. She looks like a man in drag, like she's wearing a bad Halloween costume, like it's all a horrible joke.

"Maybe my hair won't fall out?" she says.

"It's okay," the woman in the wig shop says. "Insurance covers it. Ask your doctor to write a prescription for a cranial prosthesis."

"I'm a doctor," my wife says.

The wig woman looks confused. "It's okay," she says, putting another wig on my wife's head.

She buys a wig. I never see it. She brings it home and immediately puts it in the closet. "It looks like Linda Evans, like someone on *Dynasty*. I just can't do it," she says.

Her scalp begins to tingle. Her hair hurts. "It's as though someone grabbed my hair and is pulling as hard as they can."

"It's getting ready to go," I say. "It's like a time bomb. It ticks and then it blows."

"What are you, a doctor? Suddenly you know everything about cancer, about menopause, about everything?"

In the morning her hair is falling out. It is all over the pillow, all over the shower floor.

"Your hair's not really falling out," Enid says when we meet them for dinner. Enid reaches and touches her hair, sweeps her hand through it, as if to be comforting. She ends up with a handful of hair; she has pulled my wife's hair out. She tries to put it back, she furiously pats it back in place.

"Forget that I was worried about them shaving my pubic hair, how 'bout it all just went down the drain."

She looks like a rat, like something that's been chewed on and spit out, like something that someone tried to electrocute and failed. In four days she is eighty percent bald.

She stands before me naked. "Document me."

I take pictures. I take the film to one of those special stores that has a sign in the window—we don't censor.

I give her a baseball cap to wear to work. Every day she goes to work, she will not miss a day, no matter what.

I, on the other hand, can't work. Since this happened, my work has been nonexistent. I spend my day as the holder of the feelings, the keeper of sensation.

"It's not my fault," she says. "What the hell do you do all day while I'm at the hospital?"

Recuperate.

She wears the baseball cap for a week and then takes a razor, shaves the few scraggly hairs that remain, and goes to work bald, without a hat, without a wig—starkers.

There's something both admirable and aggressive about her baldness, as if she's saying to everyone—I have cancer and you have to deal with it.

"How do you feel?" I ask at night when she comes home from the hospital.

"I feel nothing."

"How can you feel nothing?"

"I am made of steel and wood," she says happily.

As we're falling asleep she tells me a story. "It's true, it happened as I was walking to the hospital. I accidentally bumped into someone on the sidewalk. Excuse me, I said and continued on. He ran after me, 'Excuse me, boy. Excuse me, boy. You knocked my comb out of my hand and I want you to go back and pick it up.' I turned around—we bumped into each other, I said excuse me, and that will have to suffice. 'You knocked it out of my hand on purpose, white boy.' I said, I am not a boy. 'Then what are you—Cancer Man? Or are you just a bitch? A bald fucking bitch.' I wheeled around and chased him. You fucking crazy ass, I screamed. You fucking crazy ass. I screamed it about four times. He's lucky I didn't fucking kill him," she says.

I am thinking she's lost her mind. I'm thinking she's lucky he didn't kill her.

She stands up on the bed—naked. She strikes a pose like a body builder. "Cancer Man," she says, flexing her muscles, creating a new superhero. "Cancer Man!"

Luckily she has good insurance. The bill for the surgery comes—it's itemized. They charge per part removed. Ovary $7,000, appendix $5,000, the total is $72,000 dollars. "It's all in a day's work," she says.

We are lying in bed. I am lying next to her, reading the paper.

"I want to go to a desert island, alone. I don't want to come back until this is finished," she says.

"You are on a desert island, but unfortunately you have taken me with you."

She looks at me. "It will never be finished—do you know that? I'm not going to have children and I'm going to die."

"Do you really think you're going to die?"

"Yes."

I reach for her.

"Don't," she says. "Don't go looking for trouble."

"I wasn't. I was trying to be loving."

"I don't feel loving," she says. "I don't feel physically bonded to anyone right now, including myself."

"You're pushing me away."

"I'm recovering," she says.

"It's been eighteen weeks."

Her blood counts are low. Every night for five nights, I inject her with Nupagen to increase the white blood cells. She teaches me how to prepare the injection, how to push the needle into the muscle of her leg. Every time I inject her, I apologize.

"For what?" she asks.

"Hurting you."

"Forget it," she says, disposing of the needle.

"Could I have a hug?" I ask.

She glares at me. "Why do you persist? Why do you keep asking me for things I can't do, things I can't give?"

"A hug?"

"I can't give you one."

"Anyone can give a hug. I can get a hug from the doorman."

"Then do," she says. "I need to be married to someone who is like a potted plant, someone who needs nothing."

"Water?"

"Very little, someone who is like a cactus or an orchid."

"It's like you're refusing to be human," I tell her.

"I have no interest in being human."

This is information I should be paying attention to. She is telling me something and I'm not listening. I don't believe what she is saying.

I go to dinner with Eric and Enid alone.

"It's strange," they say. "You'd think the cancer would soften her, make her more appreciative. You'd think it would make her stop and think about what she wants to do with the rest of her life. When you ask her, what does she say?" Eric and Enid want to know.

"Nothing. She says she wants nothing, she has no needs or desires. She says she has nothing to give."

Eric and Enid shake their heads. "What are you going to do?"

I shrug. None of this is new, none of this is just because she has cancer—that's important to keep in mind, this is exactly the way she always was, only more so.

A few days later a woman calls; she and her husband are people we see occasionally.

"Hi, how are you, how's Tom?" I ask.

"He's a fucking asshole," she says. "Haven't you heard? He left me."

"When?"

"About two weeks ago. I thought you would have known."

"I'm a little out of it."

"Anyway, I'm calling to see if you'd like to have lunch."

"Lunch, sure. Lunch would be good."

At lunch she is a little flirty, which is fine, it's nice actually, it's been a long time since someone flirted with me. In the end, when we're having coffee, she spills the beans. "So I guess you're wondering why I called you?"

"I guess," I say, although I'm perfectly pleased to be having lunch, to be listening to someone else's troubles.

"I heard your wife was sick, I figured you're not getting a lot of sex, and I thought we could have an affair."

I don't know which part is worse, the complete lack of seduction, the fact that she mentions my wife not being well, the idea that my wife's illness would make me want to sleep with her, her stun gun bluntness—it's all too much.

"What do you think? Am I repulsive? Thoroughly disgusting? Is it the craziest thing you ever heard?"

"I'm very busy," I say, not knowing what to say, not wanting to be offensive, or seem to have taken offense. "I'm just very busy."

My wife comes home from work. "Someone came in today—he reminded me of you."

"What was his problem?"

"He jumped out the window."

"Dead?"

"Yes," she says, washing her hands in the kitchen sink.

"Was he dead when he got to you?" There's something in her tone that makes me wonder, did she kill him?

"Pretty much."

"What part reminded you of me?"

"He was having an argument with his wife," she says. "Imagine her standing in the living room, in the middle of a sentence, and out the window he goes. Imagine her not having a chance to finish her thought?"

"Yes, imagine, not being able to have the last word. Did she try to stop him?" I ask.

"I don't know," my wife says. "I didn't get to read the police report. I just thought you'd find it interesting."

"What do you want for dinner?"

"Nothing," she says. "I'm not hungry."

"You have to eat something."

"Why? I have cancer. I can do whatever I want."

Something has to happen.

I buy tickets to Paris. "We have to go." I invoke the magic word, "It's an *emergency*."

"It's not like I get a day off. It's not like I come home at the end of the day and I don't have cancer. It goes everywhere with me. It doesn't matter where I am, it's still me—it's me with cancer. In Paris I'll have cancer."

I dig out the maps, the guide books, everything we did on our last trip is marked with fluorescent highlighter. I am acting as though I believe that if we retrace our steps, if we return to a place where things were good, there will be an automatic correction, a psychic chiropractic event, which will put everything into alignment.

I gather provisions for the plane, fresh fruit, water, magazines, the smoke hoods. It's a little-known fact, smoke inhalation is a major cause of death on airplanes.

"What's the point," she says, throwing a few things into a suitcase. "You can do everything and think you're prepared, but you don't know what's going to happen. You don't see what's coming until it hits you in the face."

She points at someone outside. "See that idiot crossing the street in front of the truck—why doesn't he have cancer?"

She lifts her suitcase—too heavy. She takes things out. She leaves her smoke hood on the bed. "If the plane fills with smoke, I'm going to be so happy," she says. "I'm going to breathe deeply, I'm going to be the first to die."

I stuff the smoke hood into my suitcase, along with her raincoat, her extra shoes, and vitamin C drops. I lift the suitcases, I feel like a pack animal, a sherpa.

In France, the customs people are not used to seeing bald women. They call her "sir."

"Sir, you're next, sir. Sir, please step over here, sir."

My wife is my husband. She loves it. She smiles. She catches my eye and strikes a subdued version of the super hero/body builder pose, flexing. "Cancer Man," she says.

"And what is the purpose of your visit to France?" the inspector asks. "Business or pleasure?"

"Reconciliation," I say, watching her—Cancer Man.

"Business or pleasure?"

"Pleasure."

Paris is my fantasy, my last-ditch effort to reclaim my marriage, myself, my wife.

As we are checking into the hotel, I remind her of our previous visit—the chef cut himself, his finger was severed, she saved it, and they were able to reattach it. "You made medical history. Remember the beautiful dinner they threw in your honor."

"It was supposed to be a vacation," she says.

The bellman takes us to our room—there's a big basket of fruit, bottles of Champagne and Evian with a note from the concierge welcoming us.

"It's not as nice as it used to be," she says, already disappointed. She opens the Evian and drinks. Her lips curl. "Even the water tastes bad."

"Maybe it's you. Maybe the water is fine. Is it possible you're wrong?"

"We see things differently," she says, meaning she's right, I'm wrong.

"Are you in an especially bad mood, or is it just the cancer?" I ask.

"Maybe it's you?" she says.

We walk, across the river and down by the Louvre. There could be nothing better, nothing more perfect, and yet I am suddenly hating Paris—the beauty, the fineness of it is dwarfed by her foul humor. I realize there will be no saving it, no moment of reconciliation, redemption. Everything is irredeemably awful and getting worse.

"If you're so unhappy, why don't you leave?" I ask her.

"I keep thinking you'll change."

"If I changed any more I can't imagine who I'd be."

"Well, if I'm such a bitch, why do you stay?"

"It's my job, it's my calling to stay with you, to soften you."

"I absolutely do not want to be softer, I don't want to give another inch."

She trips on a cobblestone, I reach for her elbow, to steady her, and instead unbalance myself. She fails to catch me. I fall and recover quickly.

"Imagine how I feel," she says. "I am a doctor and I can't fix it. I can't fix me, I can't fix you—what a lousy doctor."

"I'm losing you," I say.

"I've lost myself. Look at me—do I look like me?"

"You act like yourself."

"I act like myself because I have to, because people are counting on me."

"I'm counting on you."

"Stop counting."

All along the Tuileries there are Ferris wheels—the world's largest Ferris wheel is set up in the middle.

"Let's go," I say, taking her hand and pulling her toward them.

"I don't like rides."

"It's not much of a ride. It's like a carousel, only vertical. Live a little."

She gets on. There are no seat belts, no safety bars. I say nothing. I am hoping she won't notice.

"How is it going to end?" I ask while we're waiting for the wheel to spin.

"I die in the end."

The ride takes off, climbing, pulling us up and over. We are flying, soaring; the city unfolds. It is breathtaking and higher than I thought. And faster. There is always a moment on any ride when you think it is too fast, too high, too far, too wide, and that you will not survive. And then there is the exhilaration of surviving, the thrill of having lived through it and immediately you want to go around again.

"I have never been so unhappy in my life," my wife says when we're near the top. "It's not just the cancer, I was unhappy before the cancer. We were having a very hard time. We don't get along, we're a bad match. Do you agree?"

"Yes," I say. "We're a really bad match, but we're such a good bad match it seems impossible to let it go."

"We're stuck," she says.

"You bet," I say.

"No. I mean the ride, the ride isn't moving."

"It's not stuck, it's just stopped. It stops along the way."

She begins to cry. "It's all your fault. I hate you. And I still have to deal with you. Every day I have to look at you."

"No, you don't. You don't have to deal with me if you don't want to."

She stops crying and looks at me. "What are you going to do, jump?"

"The rest of your life, or my life, however long or short, should not be miserable. It can't go on this way."

163

"We could both kill ourselves," she says.

"How about we separate?"

I am being more grown-up than I am capable of being. I am terrified of being without her, but either way, it's death.

The ride lurches forward.

I came to Paris wanting to pull things together and suddenly I am desperate to be away from her. If this doesn't stop now, it will never stop, it will go on forever. She will be dying of her cancer and we will still be fighting. I begin to panic, to feel I can't breathe. I am suffocating; I have to get away.

"Where does it end?"

"How about we say good-bye?"

"And then what? We have opera tickets."

I cannot tell her I am going. I have to sneak away, to tiptoe out backwards. I have to make my own arrangements.

We stop talking. We're hanging in mid-air, suspended. We have run out of things to say. When the ride circles down, the silence becomes more definitive.

I begin to make my plan. In truth, I have no idea what I am doing. All afternoon, everywhere we go, I cash traveler's checks, I get cash advances, I have about five thousand dollars' worth of francs stuffed in my pocket. I want to be able to leave without a trace, I want to be able to buy myself out of whatever trouble I get into. I am hysterical and giddy all at once.

We are having an early dinner on our way to the opera.

I time my break for just after the coffee comes. "Oops," I say, feeling my pockets. "I forgot my opera glasses."

"Really?" she says. "I thought you had them when we went out."

"They must be at the hotel. You go on ahead, I'll run back. You know I hate not being able to see."

She takes her ticket. "Hurry," she says. "I hate it when you're late."

This is the bravest thing I have ever done. I go back to the hotel and pack my bag. I am going to get out. I am going to

fly away. I may never come back. I will begin again, as someone else—unrecognizable.

I move to lift the bag off the bed, I pull it up and my knee
goes out. I start to fall but catch myself. I pull at the bag and
take a step—too heavy. I will have to go without it. I will have
to leave everything behind. I drop the bag, but still I am
falling, folding, collapsing. There is pain, searing, spreading,
pouring, hot and cold, like water down my back, down my
legs.

I am lying on the floor, thinking that if I stay calm, if I can
just find my breath, and follow my breath, it will pass. I lie
there waiting for the paralysis to recede.

I am afraid of it being over and yet she has given me no
choice, she has systematically withdrawn life support: sex
and conversation. The problem is that, despite this, she is the
one I want.

There is a knock at the door. I know it is not her, it is too
soon for it to be her.

"Entrez," I call out.

The maid opens the door, she holds the DO NOT DISTURB
sign in her hand. "Ooooff," she says, seeing me on the floor.
"Do you need the doctor?"

I am not sure if she means my wife or a doctor other than
my wife.

"No."

She takes a towel from her cart and props it under my
head. She takes a spare blanket from the closet and covers me
with it. She opens the Champagne and pours me a glass, tilt-
ing my head up so I can sip. She goes to her cart and gets a
stack of night chocolates and sits beside me, feeding me
Champagne and chocolate, stroking my forehead.

The phone in the room rings, we ignore it. She refills my
glass. She takes my socks off and rubs my feet. She unbuttons
my shirt and rubs my chest. I am getting a little drunk. I am
just beginning to relax and then there is another knock, a
knock my body recognizes before I am fully awake. Every-

thing tightens. My back pulls tighter still, any sensation below my knees drops off.

"I thought something horrible happened to you, I've been calling and calling the room, why haven't you answered? I thought you'd killed yourself."

The maid excuses herself. She goes into the bathroom and gets me a cool washcloth.

"What are you doing?" my wife asks.

There is nothing I can say.

"Knock off the mummy routine. What exactly are you doing? Were you trying to run away and then you chickened out? Say something."

To talk would be to continue; for the moment I am silenced. I am a potted plant, and still that is not good enough for her.

"He is paralyzed," the maid says.

"He is not paralyzed. I am his wife, I am a doctor. I would know if there was something really wrong."

THE WEATHER OUTSIDE IS SUNNY
AND BRIGHT

In the morning there are marks where the pillow touched his face, where his T-shirt wrinkled against his back, from the waistband of his underwear, elastic indentations, ghostly traces. He peels off the socks he wore to sleep, the pattern is like a picket fence. With her fingernail she writes on his chest, Milk, Butter, Eggs, Sugar. The invisible ink of her finger rises up like a welt. In the shower it becomes perfectly clear—dermatographism. For the moment he is a walking grocery list— it will fade within the hour.

"I dreamed I was in the eighteenth century, having tea in a very elaborate cup." He is a clockmaker lost in time, keeping track of the seconds, fascinated by the beats, hours passing, future becoming past. "And you? How did you sleep?"

"I dreamed the building was sealed, there were no doors, no windows, no way in or out, nothing to knock, nothing to ring, nothing to bang against," she says. "The house of glass was suddenly all solid walls."

"You are what you dream," he says.

"It's true." She puts on her shoes, slipping a small piece of lead into both left and right, to keep her mind from wandering, to keep herself steady. "I'm late," she says.

"You have a feather," he reaches out to pluck something poking out of her skin. She sometimes gets feathers; they erupt as pimples and then a hard quill like a splinter presses through the same way a feather sticks through the ticking of a pillow or the seat of a sofa.

"Is that the only one?" she asks.

He searches her arms and legs and pulls out a couple more. "All plucked and ready to go," he says.

"Thanks," she says. "Don't forget the groceries."

He nods. "Yesterday there was a fox in the woods; for a minute I thought it was you. I went to say hello and it gave me an angry eye—you're not angry with me, are you?"

"It wasn't me. I was at the office all day."

On her way out the door she puts a clump of dirt in her mouth, presses a pumpkin seed in, and swallows for good luck.

"Drive carefully," he says. He sprinkles fish food into the pond of koi, flips a penny in, and waves good-bye.

Outside, the lawns are being watered, the garden men are going around with their weed whackers, trimming, pruning. Everything is shape and order. There is the *tsk, tsk, tsk* hissing sound as the sprinklers spit water over the grass.

The landscape winding down the hill reminds her of Japan, of Scotland, of another country in another time. There are big rocks, boulders, and sand; a desert, dense vegetation clinging to the sides of craggy hills. There are palm trees, and date trees, and orange and lemon groves.

There is fog in the canyons, a hint of blue sky at the top of the hill. The weather changes from block to block—it is impossible to know what kind of day it will be.

She sits at her desk, pouring over drawings, reading between the lines. Her workspace is industrial, minimal: a skylight, an exposed wooden ceiling, furniture from an old factory.

Four pens on her desk, ten paper clips, a plastic spoon. Twenty steps from her desk to the door. She is always counting. There is something reassuring about numbers, she does math in her head, math to keep herself entertained, to keep everything in order.

Magnetized, she attracts things—right now she has a paper clip on the tip of every finger, like press-on nails. When she's bored, she decorates herself in loose change, quarters all up and down her arms. Her watch clings to her wrist, synched with her heartbeat. Her pulse an even sixty beats per minute. When she exercises, she takes the watch off, afraid of breaking time.

"You are a magnetic, highly influential person," a psychic once told her. "People and things are drawn to you."

Making herself a cup of tea, she puts in a pinch of catnip—it makes her pleasant and playful. When she smiles, a thin line of soil at her gumline is easily mistaken for a tobacco stain.

Architectural forensics is her field—why buildings do what they do. Often called upon as an expert witness, she is known as "X-ray specs" for her ability to read the inanimate, to intuit what transformed it, to find the otherwise invisible marks of what happened and why. She is the one you want to call when there is a problem to solve—cracking, sinking, the seemingly inexplicable.

Her first appointment is a disaster. From the moment she's out of the car, she's uncomfortable. She has flashes of things she doesn't want to know—other people's memories. The owner meets her in the parking lot. "It's an insurance question. It's a liability question. It's a question of who's going to pay," he tells her, as he sweeps a single long lock of hair across his bald head and sweat pastes it down.

"There's something wrong with your facade," she tells him.

"A partial collapse," the owner says, pointing at the damage.

She circles the building. If the man weren't watching, she would make herself into a squirrel or a bee and get inside it. She would get between the walls, between what was original and what was applied later. Instead, she simply uses an extension rod and pokes at things.

The owner moves to let her into the building.

"Old keys have more power than new," she says as the man fumbles.

"Could I have seen it coming? Could I have known? There was no warning."

"Or was there? Just because you don't see it doesn't mean it isn't there—there is something called willful blindness."

"Is that a legal term?" he asks nervously.

"No," she says, getting back into her car.

"Don't you need to get inside?" he asks.

"I've seen enough," she says.

"A woman died," the man confesses.

She already knows.

A click of the shutter. Her day is spent looking, taking notes with her camera, making permanent what she sees in her mind's eye. She is a special kind of anthropologist, studying what can't be touched or seen. She drives, moving through air, counting the molecules.

She is thinking of shapes—volumes, groined vaults of gothic cathedrals, cable roofs, tents. She is thinking of different kinds of ceilings. She is noticing there is a lot of smog, a suffocating layer.

As a child she fell down a well, like something out of a nursery rhyme. "That explains it," her teachers used to say, but it didn't. One thing had nothing to do with the next, except that she was curious, always curious, but there was more to it than that.

She walks with a slight limp, an unnecessary reminder. She remembers the well, she remembers thinking that she saw something there—she was eight, almost nine—leaning over, catching a glimpse of something in the corner of her eye.

She remembers screaming as she fell, the echo of her voice swelling the well. Wedged, her leg oddly bent. She remembers silence.

And she remembers her mother shouting down to her,

"Imagine you are a bird, a winged thing, and push yourself up. Imagine you are a flower, growing. Imagine you are something that can scale a stony wall." Her mother shouting; many, many hours of firemen and ropes. She remembers thinking she would fall to the center of the earth, she remembers the blackness. And her picture in all the papers.

After that, while she was resting in bed, her broken leg healing, her mother would hold her hand and stroke it. "What does it feel like to be a kitten? What does a little kitten hear or see?" And slowly her features would change and she would be a little kitten-headed girl. "And what does a kitten do with her paws?" her mother would ask, stroking her hand, and little furry mitts would appear.

"You're very special," her mother would say. "When you fell down the well, you didn't know that."

She nods, still not sure what her mother is getting at— aren't all little girls special?

"Some children are born with a fine coating of hair, but when you were born you had feathers—that's how I knew. When you were living inside me you were a duck, splashing. You know what a good swimmer you are—you had a lot of practice."

Looking out over the city, she receives a thousand messages at once, a life of information.

The next stop is more promising—a developer wants her opinion about where to build his building.

"You come highly recommended," the man says, unrolling his plans across the hood of her car.

She reads them. Her eyes are like sea water, Mediterranean blue. When you look at her you have the distinct sense that she's right.

"If I were you," she says, "I'd build in reverse, I'd build into the hill, and then on the hill install a big mirror and situate it so that it gives you a view on both sides. Put the parking lot above rather than below. You'll get a double view, an interesting courtyard effect, and more protection from the wind."

"The wind?"

She opens her trunk, takes out a white flag and holds it up. The flag is instantly billowing. "It's windier than you think, and when you add a new building you could end up creating a wind tunnel: the Venturi Effect—in certain configurations, the wind speed increases."

"I never heard of that."

She puts the flag back in her trunk.

"What else you got in there?" he says, peering in.

Shovel, gallon of water, long green garden hose, ladder, rope, rubber gloves, knee pads. She is always climbing, swinging, getting on top, going under.

She bends to sift through the soil. "This looks sandy. Sandy soil has a liquefaction factor," she says. "In an earthquake it's not the 'this' that gets you," she says, moving her arm from side to side. "It's the 'this.'" She pumps her hand up and down. "A lot of it has to do with what kind of soil is down below."

The man scoops up some dirt. "Is that a good thing?"

"It's a good thing you know about it and can plan accordingly. It's all about what rock you're on."

"I appreciate your insight." He shakes her hand. His handshake is firm. "Thank you."

All day the building collapse haunts her, she keeps seeing the sticky guy sweeping sweaty strands of hair across his scalp, patting them down. He is slimy, slithering, slipping in and out of lies. She has the sensation of great weight, of something falling on her, crushing her. She feels out of breath but she keeps moving to keep herself from feeling trapped.

She stops for lunch at the health food store. The boy behind the counter sings a song he's just written. "I'm here now," he says. "But it's just temporary." Everyone is something else, everyone wants something more.

She is back at the office. People bring her samples of materials, combinations of things. They want to know what goes with what. What brings success, power? What juxtapositions spell trouble? What do you think of titanium? Curved surfaces? How much does a building really need to breathe? They want to know how she knows what she knows. "Did you study Feng Shui?"

The temperature creeps up—the air is still, like the steady baking heat of an oven, unrelenting, broken only by the shadow of a cloud passing over.

In the afternoon, she visits her mother. The doors of the nursing home open automatically; a cool disinfectant smell pours out. Vacuum sealed, frozen in time. There is an easel by the main desk: GOOD AFTERNOON. THE YEAR IS 2002. TODAY IS WEDNESDAY, MAY 16TH. THE WEATHER OUTSIDE IS SUNNY AND BRIGHT. Her mother's unit is behind a locked door. There is a sign on the wall: "Look as you are leaving, make sure no one follows you."

Her mother doesn't know her anymore. It happened over the course of a year. The first time she pretended it was a mistake—of course you know me, she said. And her mother seemed to catch herself, but then it happened again, it happened more, and then sometimes she knew her, sometimes she didn't—and then she didn't.

Every day, she visits. She brings her camera, she takes a picture. It is her way of dealing with the devastation, the rug pulled out from under.

"Hello," she says, walking into the room.

"Hello," her mother repeats, a parrot, echoing.

"How are you today?"

"How are you today?"

"I'm good," she sits at the edge of her mother's bed, unfastening her mother's long braids, brushing her hair.

"Remind me," her mother says. "Who are you?"

"I'm your daughter."

"What makes you so sure?"

"Because I remember you," she says.

"From before?" her mother asks.

She nods.

"My sock is itching," her mother says, rubbing the tag around her ankle. All the residents are tagged—an alarm goes off if they wander out—the tag leg is alternated, but it remains an irritant.

"What can we do?" the nurse says. "We don't want to lose anyone, do we?"

She rubs lotion on her mother's leg. She puts a chestnut in her mother's pocket just as she once saw her mother do to her grandmother—to ward off backaches. She puts an orange she picked this morning on the nightstand, resting on a bed of clover. Protection, luck, vision.

She takes her mother for a walk in the wandering garden, an inconspicuous circle, you always end where you begin—it guarantees no one gets lost.

"Let me take your picture," she says, posing her mother by some flowering vines. "You look very pretty."

"You look very pretty," her mother says.

Holding hands, they walk around and around.

"I hope you remember the way home," her mother says.

"Remember when I fell in the well? Remember when you told me how strong I was and that I had to put my mind to it?"

Her mother nods. "I used to know something," her mother says. "Have you always had a limp?"

She visits her mother and then visits the other women up and down the hall. "Imagine us," they say, "sitting here, like lame ducks. We see it all. There but for the grace, go I."

When her mother is gone, she will continue to visit the unvisited. Every day she touches them; they are wrinkly, covered in barnacles and scars, filled with secret histories, things no one will know. She touches them and their stories unfold.

"You look familiar," one of them says. "I know you from somewhere."

"You know me from here," she says.

"Where was I before this?" the woman asks. "Does anyone know where I am? I'm missing," she says.

Another woman runs through the rooms, opening all the dresser drawers, searching.

"What are you looking for?" the nurse asks.

"I am looking for something," she says in tears. "That's what I'm looking for."

"Describe it to me," she says, laying her hand on the woman's arm.

"I don't know exactly what it is. I'm looking for something that I recognize. I think maybe I'm in the wrong place. If I could find something familiar I would know where I belong."

She brings them pictures of themselves.

"Is this who I am?" they say.

She nods.

"Sexy, aren't I?"

The sea. She drives to the ocean and parks. She takes a picture. She finds the fact that she is not the only one moving calming.

She is a navigator, a mover, a shifter. She has flown as a gull over the ocean, she has dived deep as a whale, she has spent an afternoon as a jellyfish floating, as an evergreen with the breeze tickling her skin, she has spent two days as water and found it difficult to recover. A seer, she is in constant motion, trying to figure out what comes next.

It is early evening. The sky is charcoal, powdery black. She is a coyote at the edge of the grass: her spine elongated, her nose pushing forward, and her skull rolling back. There is something slippery about the coyote—a million

THINGS YOU SHOULD KNOW

years of motion, of shifting to accommodate, keeping a fluid boundary—she is coated in a viscous watery solution.

She digs through the bushes. There is a girl in the backyard, floating alone on a raft in the water. She walks to the pool, dips her tongue into the water, and sips.

She hears the girl's mother and father in the house. Shouting.

"What am I to you?" her mother says.

"It's the same thing, always the same thing, blah, blah, blah," her father says.

"Your life is a movie," the coyote tells the girl. "It's not entirely real."

"Tell me about it," the girl says.

The coyote starts to change again, to shift. Her skin goes dark, it goes tan, deep like honey and then crisper brown, as if it is burning, and then darker still, toward black. Downy feathers start to appear, and then longer feathers, like quills. Her feet turn orange, fold in, and web. A duck, a big black duck, like a dog, but a duck. The duck jumps into the pool and paddles toward the girl.

They float in silence.

Suddenly, the duck lifts her head as if alerted. She pumps her wings. Her body is changing again, she is trading her feathers for fur, a black mask appears around her eyes, her bill becomes a snout. She is standing on the flagstone by the pool, a raccoon with orange webbed feet. She waddles off into the night.

There is a tremor. The lights in the house flicker, the alarm goes off. In the pool the water shifts, a small tidal wave sweeps from one end to the other, splashing up onto the concrete.

She hurries back to the car, shifting back into herself. She rushes toward home. There is a report of the tremor on the radio news, "A little rock-and-roll action this afternoon for you folks out there," the disc jockey says. "The freeways are stop and go, while crews are checking for damage." She takes surface roads, afraid of the highways, the overpasses, the spaghetti after a quake.

She pulls into the driveway, the house is still standing, nothing seems terribly wrong.

Every day she carries a raw egg in her pocket, to collect the negative flow of energy—it acts like a sponge, absorbing it, pulling it away from her. At the end of the day she smashes it back to earth, the front yard is littered with white eggshells.

Her key doesn't work, the small rumble must have caused a shifting of the tumblers, a loosening of the lock, the key goes in but won't turn. She is knocking, she is ringing the bell, going back to the car and tooting the horn.

"I couldn't get in," she says when Ben opens the door.

"The lock is broken," he says, turning the knob. "Your hair is wet."

"I stopped for a swim."

"And I think you lost your shoes." He points at her bare feet. They are almost back to normal, but the three middle toes remain for the moment webbed and orange. "I rushed back. Are you all right?" she asks him.

"Fine. Everything is fine. The front window has a crack," he says.

"Stress fracture," she says, "Did they call?"

He nods. "About fifteen minutes ago. I reported vibration and minor damage."

In their backyard there is a global positioning monument, a long probe sunk deep into the earth. Every thirty seconds one of five satellites registers the position of the monument, measuring the motion in scientific millimeters. There are hundreds of them, up and down the state. She and Ben get a tax credit for "the friendly use of land." And every time there's an event, the phone rings. "Just checking in."

When she stands near the monument, when she focuses on it, she can feel the satellite connecting, a gentle pull for a fraction of a second, a tugging at the marrow.

"There are footprints," Ben says, pointing out the press of a paw on the loamy ground behind the house. "I'm thinking dog or deer."

"Mountain lion," she says, bending to sniff the print, pressing her hand into the dirt over it.

Ben takes a dry towel and rubs her hair—at the roots her hair is fluorescent orange, the rest is brunette. The color changes according to her mood, or, more accurately, her emotional temperature. The only way she can disguise her feelings or not look like a clown is to dye her long locks. "Are you especially frightened?"

"The tremor threw me," she says. "Do I need a dye job?"

He nods. "You're bright orange."

She is cleaning her brush, her comb, saving the strands, spinning and weaving a Technicolor carpet.

"Did you go out today?" She notices that all the grocery bags on the counter are from iDot.com, the online food store—type in your list and your groceries are at the door within an hour.

"The pollen was high," he says. "The air was bad. I stayed inside, working. I made you a wonderful puzzle."

Ben is perfecting a kind of time-sensitive material, a puzzle that shifts so that the image changes as you are piecing it together. Every day he downloads photographs and turns them into something new. This time it's a picture of the sky at twilight, a single cloud. As they put the pieces together, the blue deepens; it becomes an image of the night sky and, as more of the pieces fit, a small plane flies across the sky, moving silently from piece to piece.

In every room there is a clock; Ben likes listening to the

tick, tock, tripping of the hands as he travels from room to room, as sound shifts, time bends.

He runs her a warm bath and sits by the edge while she soaks—ever since the fall in the well, she can't bear to be in water alone.

"Benjamin, are you still thinking you can stop time?" she asks as he washes her back.

"I'm working on it," he says.

"How well do you know me?"

"Very well," he says, kissing her. Her skin is the skin of youth, of constant rejuvenation, delicate, opalescent, like mother of pearl.

"Is there a beginning or an end?"

"No beginning or end in sight—infinity."

Out of the bath, he wraps a towel around her.

He presses his mouth to her skin, telling her stories.

Her heart races, the watch on her arm ticks faster. She begins to shift, to change; first she is the coyote, then a zebra, a mare, and a man. Her bones are liquid, pouring. She is laughing, crying in ten different languages, barking and baying. His hands slide over her skin, her coat, her fur, her scales, her flippers and fins. He is sucking the toes of a gorilla, kissing the ear of a seal. She is thick and thin, liquid and solid.

They are moving through time: lying on pelts in a cave, in a hand-carved bed in a palace, nomads crossing the desert, calico pioneers in a log cabin, they are on a ship, in a high-rise, on the ice in an igloo. Their cells are assembling and dis-assembling. They are flying through history. She is a cloud, vapor and texture. She is rain and sky and she is always and inescapably herself.

"Is that still you?" he asks. "I never know if you're really in there."

"It's me," she says, sliding back into herself. "In the end, it is always me."

THE FORMER FIRST LADY AND
THE FOOTBALL HERO

The white van accelerates. He is in back, strapped in, seat-belted, shoulder-harnessed, sitting between two men in suits. She, too, is supposed to be in back, but she is up front, next to the driver. Wherever they go, she is always up front—she gets carsick.

There are escort cars front and rear, small unmarked sedans—white on the West Coast, black on the East.

"Trash day," one of the agents in the back seat says, trying to make conversation. All along the curb are large black plastic trash cans and blue recycle bins. The path is narrow, the van takes the curves broadly, swinging wide, as though it owns the road.

Something happens; there is a subtle shift, a tremor in the tectonic plates below, and the trash cans begin to roll. They pick up speed, careening downhill toward the motorcade.

"Incoming on the right," the agent shouts.

The lead car acts like a tank, taking the hit head on, the trash can explodes, showering the convoy with debris: empty Tropicana containers, Stouffer's tins, used Bounty. Something red gets stuck on the van's antenna and starts flapping like a flag.

"Son of a bitch," she says.

In the lead car, an agent whips a flashing light out of the glove compartment, slaps it down on the roof, and they take off, accelerating rapidly.

The motorcade speeds in through the main gate. Agents hover in the driveway and along the perimeter, on alert, guns drawn.

"The Hummingbird has landed. The package has been returned. We are at sea level." The agents speak into their lapels.

The gates automatically pull closed.

"What the hell was that—terrorists on St. Cloud Road?" she asks.

"Earthquake," the agent says. "We're confirming it now." He presses his ear bud deeper into his ear.

"Are you all right, sir?" they ask, helping him out of the van.

"Fit as a fiddle," he says. "That was one hell of a ride, let's saddle her up and go out again."

His eye catches the shiny red fabric stuck on the antenna. He lifts it off with his index finger, twirling it through the air—bright red panties, hooked on their lacy trim. The underpants fly off his finger and land on the gravel. Whee.

"Where are we?" he asks, kicking gravel in the driveway. "You call this a quarry? Who's directing this picture? What the hell kind of a movie is this? The set is a shambles."

The problem isn't taking him out, it's bringing him back.

"Home," she says.

"Well, it's no White House, that's for sure." He pushes up his sleeve and picks at the Band-Aid covering the spot where they injected the contrast.

Earlier, at the doctor's office, two agents waited in the exam room with him, doing card tricks, while she met with Dr. Sibley.

"How are you?" Sibley asks when she sat down.

"Fine. I'm always fine, you know that."

"Are you able to get out at all?"

She nods. "Absolutely. I had lunch at Chasens with the girls earlier this week."

There is a pause. Chasens closed several years ago. "Nothing is what it used to be," she says, catching herself. "How's he?"

Dr. Sibley turns on the light boxes. He taps his pencil against the films. "Shrinking," he says. "The brain is getting smaller."

She nods.

"Does he seem different to you? Are there sleep disturbances? Does he wander? Has he ever gotten combative? Paranoid?"

"He's fine," she says.

Now he stands in the driveway, hands on his hips. Behind him is blue sky. There is another tremor, the ground vibrates, shivers beneath his feet.

"I love that," he says. "It reminds me of a carnival ride."

She puts her arm through his and leads him into the house.

"I don't know what you're thinking," he says, "but any which way, you've got the wrong idea."

She smiles and squeezes his arm. "We'll see." Soledad, the housekeeper, rings a bell.

"This must be lunch," he says when Soledad puts a bowl of soup in front of him. Every day they have the same thing— routine prevents confusion, and besides they like it that way; they have always liked it that way.

If you feed him something different, if you give him a nice big chef's salad, he gets confused. "Did they run out of bread? What the hell kind of commissary is this?"

"What's the story with Sibley?" he asks, lifting his bowl, sipping from the edge.

She hands him a spoon. She motions to him how to use it. He continues drinking from the bowl.

"He doesn't seem to be getting me any work. Every week I see him; squeeze this, lift that, testing me to see if I've still got the juice. But then he does nothing for me. Maybe we should fire him and get someone new. How about the folks over at William Morris—there has to be someone good there. How about Swifty Lazar, I always thought he was a character." He puts the bowl down.

"Swifty's dead."

"Is he? Well, then, he's not much better than Sibley." He trails off. "Who am I?" he asks her.

"You're my man," she says.

"Well, they certainly did a good job when they cast you as my wife—whose idea was that?"

"Dore Schary," she says.

He nods. "And who am I really?"

"Who would you like to be?"

They sit in silence. "May I be excused?"

She nods. He gets up from the table and heads down the hall toward his office. Every afternoon he writes letters and pays bills. He uses an out-of-date checkbook and one-cent stamps, sometimes a whole sheet on a single envelope. He spits on the back of the sheet of stamps, rubs the spit around, and wraps the letter in postage.

"Would you like me to mail that?" she asks when he is done.

"This one's for you," he often says, handing her an envelope.

"I look forward to receiving it," she says, taking the envelope from him.

Once, a letter was accidentally mailed—a five-thousand-dollar donation to a Palestinian Naturalists' Organization—Nude in the Desert.

Every day he writes her a letter. His handwriting is unsteady and she can't always read every word, but she tries.

Mommy—

I see you. I love you always. Love, Me.

He smiles. There are moments when she sees a glimmer, the shine that tells her he's in there, and then it is gone.

"Lucky?" he says.

"Lucky's no more," she says.

"Lucy?"

She shakes her head. "That was a long time ago," she says. "Lucky is long gone."

She gives him a pat on the head and a quick scratch behind the ears. "Errands to run," she says. "I'm leaving you with Philip."

"Philip?"

"The pool boy," she says.

"Is Philip the same as Bennett?" Bennett was his bodyguard and chauffeur from gubernatorial days.

"Yes," she says.

"Well, why don't you just say so? What's all the mystery? Why don't you call him Bennett?"

"I don't want to confuse him," she says.

Philip is the LPN. He fills the daily minder—pill container, doles out the herbal supplements, and gives the baths. The idea of a male nurse is so unmasculine that it sickens her. She thinks of male nurses as weaklings, serial killers, repressed homosexuals.

Philip was Dr. Sibley's idea. For a while they had part-time help, a girl in the afternoons. One afternoon she came home from shopping and asked how he was.

"He have good lunch," the girl said, followed by "Your husband have very big penis."

She found him in the sunroom with an erection. "Would you look at me," he said.

"Sometimes, as memory fades, a man becomes more aggressive, more sexual," Sibley said. "The last thing we'd want is a bastard baby claiming to be the President's child. Avoid the issue," Sibley advised. "Hire this Philip fellow. He comes highly recommended. Call him the President's personal trainer."

From the beginning, there is something about Philip that she doesn't like—something hard to put her finger on, something sticky, almost gooey, he is soft in the center like caramel.

She picks up the phone, dialing the extension for the pool house.

"Should I come in now?" Philip asks.

"Why else would I call?"

"Philip is going to give you your treatment, and then maybe you'll take a little nap."

His treatment is a bath and a massage. He has become afraid of the shower—shooting water. Every day Philip gives him a treatment.

"Don't leave me here alone," he says, grabbing at the edge of her skirt, clinging, begging her not to leave.

"I can't disappoint the people, now can I?" She pries his fingers off.

"I wouldn't be myself without you," he says rummaging around, looking for something. "Where is my list? My lines? I've got calls to make. Remind me, what's her name, with the accent? Mugs?"

"Margaret Thatcher?" Philip says.

He looks at her for confirmation. She nods.

"See you later," she says.

He picks up the phone. It automatically rings in the kitchen. In order to get an outside line you have to dial a three-digit code.

"Operator," Soledad says, picking up.

"Put me through to Mrs. Thatcher," he says.

"One moment, please," Soledad says. She makes the ring, ring sound. "Good afternoon, London here." Soledad mimics an English accent. "America calling," she says, switching back to her operator voice. "I have the President on the line."—"Jolly well, then, put him through," she says in her English accent. "You're on the line, sir, go ahead," she says.

"Margaret," he says, "she's left me, gone for good, now it's just the two of us. Are we on the same team? Are all our soldiers in a line? Are you packed and ready to go at a moment's notice? Is there enough oil? Are we on the same team? Did I just ask you that?"

When she goes, she's gone. She passes through her dressing room, freshens her face, sprays her hair, puts a red suit on, and practically runs out to the car.

Whenever she wants to be seen she wears a red suit—she has a dozen of them: Adolfo, Armani, Beene, Blass, Cassini, Dior, Galanos, Saint Laurent, Ungaro. When she goes out with him, when she goes incognito, she wears pastels. No one looks at an old woman in pastel pull-on pants.

"The Hummingbird is in the feeder." Her agents talk into their lapels.

"Where to?" Jim asks as the gate swings open.

"Let's go down to Rodeo and window-shop. Maybe we'll stop at Saks or Barney's."

Sometimes she has the men drive her to Malibu to clear her head, sometimes she goes walking down Beverly Boulevard, like a tourist attraction. Sometimes she needs to be recognized, reminded of who she is, reminded that she is not the one evaporating.

"Notify BHPD that we'll be in their jurisdiction. Anticipate R&W." They radio ahead. "R&W" stands for the vicinity of Rodeo and Wilshire.

They notify the Los Angeles field office and the local police department just in case. A couple of months ago an old drag queen paraded up and down Rodeo Drive doing a convincing imitation of her, until he asked to use the ladies' room in the GAP and came out with his skirt tucked into the back of his panty hose, flashing a flat ass and hairy thighs.

They pull into the public lot on Rodeo Drive.

The attendant waves the white car away. "Lot full," he says.

"It's okay," one of the special agents says, putting the OFFICIAL GOVT. BUSINESS placard in the window.

She carries a small purse with almost nothing in it: a lipstick, some old Republican Party pens and tie tacks to pass out as little gifts, and a bottle of liquid hand sanitizer. She is one of the few who, with good reason, regrets gloves having gone out of style—too many clammy hands in the world.

A couple comes up to her on the sidewalk. "We're here from Terre Haute," the husband says, snapping a picture of his wife with her.

"We're such big fans," the woman says. "How is the President feeling?"

"He's very strong," she says.

"We voted for you, twice," the husband says, holding up two fingers like a peace sign.

"We miss you," someone calls out.

"God bless," she says.

"I've been hoping you'd come in," Mr. Holmes in the shoe department of Saks confides. He is her regular salesman. "I'm holding some Ferragamos for you—they're on sale." He whispers as though protecting her privacy.

"There's nothing nicer than new shoes," she says, sliding into the pumps. She looks at her legs in the half mirror. "At least my ankles are still good," she says.

"You are very thin," Mr. Holmes says, shaking his head.

For years she was a six, and then a four, and now she's a two. After a lifetime of dieting she is just four sticks and a brain, her thin hair teased high, like spun caramel sugar, hard.

"The shoes are down to one-sixty but with my discount I can get them for you at one-thirty-five."

"You've always been good to me."

He knows enough to have them sent. He knows to put it on account, not to bring her the bag or the paperwork. She doesn't sign bills of sale or carry bags, and the agents need to keep their hands free.

In Barney's, she stops at the makeup counter.

"Is that really you?" the salesgirl asks.

"Yes." She glances into the magnifying mirror. Blown-up,

she looks scary, preserved like something dipped in formaldehyde. "I need something for my skin," she tells the girl.

"I've got just the thing for you," the girl pulls out a cotton ball. "May I?"

She nods. "You may."

"It goes on light." The girl dabs her face with the moisturizer. "But is has enough body to fill in any uneven spots. Your skin is lovely, you must have a good regimen."

"Smoke and mirrors," she says. "Hollywood magic."

The agents look away, their eyes, ever vigilant, scan the room. In Los Angeles, the agents dress down. They dress like golf pros—knitted short-sleeved shirts, sweaters, and permanent-press pants. They keep their guns in fanny packs under their sweaters. Their ear buds are clear plastic, like hearing aids.

"That's lovely," she says. "I'll take a jar."

A woman comes rushing across the store toward her, the agents pull in. "I heard you were here." The woman moves to kiss her on the cheek, they brush the sides of their faces, their hairdos against each other.

"You look fantastic," she says, unable to remember the woman's name—she thinks it might be Maude.

"Of course I do," the woman says. "I'm like a time machine. Every year, I intend to look five years younger. By the time I die I'll look like Jon Benet."

"Could I trouble you for an autograph?" someone interrupts, handing her a piece of paper to sign.

A woman standing off to the side pushes her little girl in the First Lady's direction. "Go and shake her hand," she says. "She used to be married to the President of the United States."

The First Lady, practiced in the art of greeting children, reaches out. The child extends a single finger, touching her like she's not quite real, like tagging her—You're it. The little girl touches the former First Lady the way you'd touch something that had cooties, the way you'd touch something just to prove you were brave enough to do it. She touches the former First Lady and then runs.

In Niketown she buys him a pair of aqua socks—they won't fall off the way his slippers do, and he can wear them everywhere: inside, outside, in the bath, to bed. She buys the aqua socks and when she realizes that no one there knows who she is, she leaves quickly.

"That was nice," she says when they are back in the car. She has started to enjoy these impromptu excursions more than official functions. At First Lady events, at library luncheons, disease breakfasts, she is under the microscope. People look at her, checking for signs of wear and tear. She keeps up a good front, she has always kept up a good front. She is careful not to be caught off guard.

"Removed from public view"—that's how they describe him on his Web site. He was removed from public view in 1988, like a statue or a painting. She will not allow him to be embarrassed, humiliated. She will not allow even the closest of their friends to see him like this. They should remember him as he was, not as he is.

Meanwhile, the two of them are in exile, self-imposed, self-preserving.

When she gets home, he is in the backyard with Philip, playing catch with a Nerf football.

"Did you miss me?" she asks.

"Liz Taylor called," he says. "She's not well. I couldn't understand a word of what she said."

Is he making it up—getting back at her for having gone out for an hour? She turns to Philip. "Did Liz Taylor really call? Do I have to call her back?"

Philip shrugs. "I don't know."

"Don't play games with me, Philip. He's not a toy, he's a man. He's a man," she repeats. "How am I supposed to know what's real? How am I supposed to know what the truth is anymore?" She shouts and then storms off to her room.

Philip and the President resume tossing the ball.

"My grip is stronger than it ever was," he says, squeezing the ball, squishing it, not realizing that it's not a real football. "I could never have done that as a young man."

Philip, running for a pass, stumbles over a lounge chair and plunges into the pool.

The President instantly dives in, wrapping his arm around Philip's neck, pulling. Philip, afraid to fight, afraid he will accidentally drown the President, guides them toward the shallow end. Philip climbs out, pulling the President out of the water, the President's arm still wrapped around his neck, choking him.

"They call me the Gripper, because I don't let go."

"I think it was Gipper, sir. They called you the Gipper, as in 'win one for the Gipper.'"

"Seventy-eight," he says.

"What's seventy-eight?"

"You're the seventy-eighth person I saved. I used to be a life guard," he says, and it is entirely true. "Hey, does that count as a bath?"

She is in her dressing room. It started as a walk-in closet and kept expanding. They broke through a wall into one of the children's bedrooms and then through another into the guest room, and now it is a dressing suite, a queen's waiting room. The carpet is Wedgwood blue, the walls white with gold trim, calmly patriotic, American royal. It is her hideaway, her fortress, command and control. She's got a computer, fax, private telephone lines, and a beauty parlor complete with a professional hair dryer. There's a divan that used to belong to Merv Griffin, photographs of her with everyone—the little lady with the big head standing next to Princess Di, Mikhail Baryshnikov, the Gorbachevs.

In her favorite velour sweat suit, she mounts the contraption—a recumbent bike with built-in screen—she can watch

TV, go online, surf the Web, write e-mails, or pedal her way down an animated bucolic country lane.

She needs to be in motion—constant motion. That's one of the reasons they call her the Hummingbird.

She logs on, checking in with her secretary—would she be willing to host a Los Angeles event with the head of the Republican Party? "OK as per N.R.," she types. She reviews a proposed album of photographs and sends a message to the chief archivist at the Presidential Library. "Dig deeper. There is a better picture of me with Raisa, also a nice one of the President and me waltzing. That should be the closing image."

She e-mails the lawyer, the business manager, the White House Alumni Office. Nothing happens without her knowledge, without her approval. She is in communication because he can't be.

Using a series of code words, she moves in further, signing into the First Ladies' Club, a project started by Barbara Bush as a way of keeping in touch; trading helpful hints about difficult subjects such as transition times—when you're not elected, you're not wanted—and standing by your man when indictments come down. They keep each other updated on their special interests, literacy, mental health, addiction, "Just Say No." They all talk about Hillary behind her back—she's a little too ambitious for them. And Hillary doesn't update her weekly "What I Did for the Good of the Country" column, instead just sending impersonal perky messages like "You Go Girl!"

The communications man has her wired up, six accounts under a variety of names—virtually untraceable. This is her solace, her salvation. This is the one place where she can be herself, or better yet, be someone else.

Under the name Edith Iowa she logs into an Alzheimer's support group.

"What do you do when they don't recognize you anymore? 'I know you from somewhere,' he says, looking at me, worried, struggling."

"He asked for more light. He kept asking more light, more light. I turned on every light in the house. He kept saying, Why is it so dark in here? Don't we pay the electric bills? I grabbed the flashlight and shined it in his face—is this enough light for you? He froze. I could see right through him and there was nothing there. Am I horrible? Did I hurt him? Is someone going to take him away? Do I ever say how much I miss him?"

She reads the stories and cries. She cries because she knows what they're talking about, because she lives in fear of the same things happening to her, because she knows that despite everything it will all come true. After a lifetime of trying not to be like everyone else, in the end she is just like everyone else.

When the doctor told them it was Alzheimer's, she thought they'd deal with it the same way they'd dealt with so many things—cancer, the assassination attempt, more cancer. But then she realized that it was not something they'd deal with, it was something she would deal with, alone. She cries because it is the erasing of a marriage, the erasing of history, as though the experiences, the memories which define her, never happened, as though nothing is real.

"How brave you are," Larry King said to her. What choice does she have?

She orders products online, things to make life easier: plastic plugs for the electric outlets, locks for the cabinets, motion detectors that turn on lamps, flood alarms, fold-down shower seats, a nonslip rubber mat for around the toilet, diapers. They arrive at a post box downtown, addressed to Western Industries. She stores them in what used to be Skipper's room. Like preparing for the arrival of an infant, she orders things in advance, she wants to have whatever he'll need on hand, she wants there to be no surprises.

Under her most brazen moniker, Lady Hawke, she goes into chat rooms, love online. The ability to flirt, to charm, is still important to her. She lists her interests as homemaking and politics. She says she's divorced with no children and puts her age at fifty-three.

—Favorite drink?

—Whiskey sour.

—Snack food?

—Caviar.

She is in correspondence with EZRIDER69, a man whose Harley has a sidecar.

—Just back from a convention in Santa Barbara—ever been there?

—Used to go all the time.

—U ride?

—Horses.

—Would love to take you for a spin in my sidecar.

—Too fast for me.

—How about on a Ferris wheel?

She feels herself blushing, it spreads through her, a liquidy warm rush.

—Dinner by the ocean?

EZ is asking her out on a date. He is a motorcyclist, a self-described leather man with a handlebar mustache, a professional hobbyist, he likes fine wines, romance, and the music of Neil Diamond.

"Not possible," she writes back. "I am not able to leave my husband. He is older and failing."

—I thought U were divorced?

She doesn't respond.

—U still there?

—Yes.

—I don't care what you are—Divorced, Married, Widowed. You could be married to the President of the United States and it wouldn't change anything—I'd still like to take you to dinner.

It changes everything. She looks at herself in the mirrored closet doors, a seventy-seven-year-old woman flirting while riding an exercise bike.

A hollow body, an elected body, a public body. The way to best shield yourself in a public life is simply to empty the inside, to have no secrets, to have nothing that requires attention, to be a vessel, a kind of figurehead, a figurine like a Staffordshire dog.

She goes to the entertainment channel and gets the latest on Brad and Jennifer. They are all in her town, down the road, around the corner. She could summon any of them and they would come quickly, out of curiosity, but she can't, she won't. Like a strange Siamese twin, the more removed he becomes the more removed she becomes.

She changes screen names again—STARPOWER—and checks in with her psychic friends, her astrological soul mates. You have to believe in something and she has always loved the stars—she is a classic Cancer, he is a prototypical Aquarius. Mercury is in retrograde, the planets are slipping out of alignment, hold on, Cancer, hold on. The planets are transiting, ascending—she works hard at keeping her houses in order.

She is pushing, always pushing. She rides for three hours, fifty miles a day. Her legs are skinny steel rods. When she's done, she showers, puts on a new outfit, and emerges refreshed.

Philip has taken him out for an hour. He still gets great pleasure from shaking hands, pressing the flesh. So, occasionally Philip dresses him up like a clown, brings him to random parking lots around town, and lets him work the crowd. In his costume, he looks like a cross between Ronald McDonald and Howdy Doody. It makes the agents very nervous.

"Mommy," he calls when he's back.

"Yes?"

"Come here." He is alone in the bedroom.

"Give me a minute," she says. "I'm powdering my nose."

She goes into the room. He beckons to her, whispering, "There's a strange man over there who keeps talking to me." He points at the television.

"That's not a strange man, that's Dan Rather—you know him from a long time ago."

"He's staring at me."

"He's not watching you, you're watching him. It's television." She goes to the TV and blows a raspberry at the screen. Dan Rather doesn't react. He keeps reporting the news.

"See," she says. "He can't see you."

"Did I like him? I don't think I liked him."

She changes the channel. "You always liked Tom Brokaw."

At twilight, he travels through time, lost in space. Terrified of the darkness, of the coming night, he follows her from room to room, at her heels, shadowing.

"It's cocktail time," she says. "Would you like a drink?"

He looks at her blankly. "Are you plotting something? Is there something I'm supposed to know? Something I'm supposed to be doing? I'm always thinking there's a paper that needs to be signed. What am I trying to remember?"

"You tell me," she says, making herself a gin and tonic.

He wanders off, in search. She stands in the living room sipping, enjoying the feel of the heavy crystal glass in her hand, running her finger over the facets, taking a moment to herself before going after him.

He is in her dressing room. He has opened every drawer and rummaged through, leaving the floor littered with clothing. Her neatly folded cashmere sweaters are scattered around the room. He's got a pair of panty hose tied around his neck like an ascot.

He has taken out a suitcase and started packing. "I've

been called away," he says, hurriedly going to and from the closet. He pulls out everything on a hanger, filling the suitcase with her dresses.

"No," she screams, seeing her beloved gowns rolled into a ball and stuffed into the bag. She rushes towards him, swatting him, pulling a Galanos out of his hands.

"It's all right," he says, going into the closet for more. "I'll be back."

Soledad, having heard the scream, charges through the door.

The place is a mess, ransacked.

"Sundowning," Philip says, arriving after the fact. "It's a common phenomena."

"Where the heck are all my clean shirts?" he asks. At the moment he is wearing four or five, like a fashion statement, piled one atop the other, buttoned so that part of each one is clearly visible. "I'm out of time."

"It's early," she says, leading him out of the room. On one of the sites she read that distraction is good for this kind of disorientation. "It's not time for you to go," she says. "Shall we dance?"

She puts on an old Glenn Miller record and they glide around the living room. The box step is embedded in his genes, he has not forgotten. She looks up at him. His chest is still deep, his pompadour still high, though graying at the roots.

"Tomorrow, when Philip gives you your bath, we'll have him dye your hair," she says, leading him into the night.

"I don't want to upset you," he whispers in her ear. "But we're being held hostage."

"By whom?" she whispers back.

"It's important that we stay calm, that we not give them any information. It's good that I'm having a little trouble with my memory, Bill Casey told me so many things that I should never have known . . . Did I have some sort of an affair?"

She pulls away from him, unsettled. "Did you?"

"I keep remembering something about getting into a lot of trouble for an affair, everyone being very unhappy with me."

"Iran Contra?"

"Who was she? A foreign girl, exotic, a beautiful dancer on a Polynesian island? Did my wife know?" he asks. "Did she forgive me? I should have known better, I should not have put us in that position, it almost cost us everything."

She changes the record to something faster, happier, a mix tape someone made her—Gloria Gaynor, Donna Summer. She spins in circles around him.

He looks at her blankly. "Have we known each other very long?"

They have dinner in the bedroom on trays in front of the television set. This is the way they've done it for years. As early as six or seven o'clock they change into their night clothes: pajamas, bathrobe, and slippers for him; a zipped red housedress with a Nehru collar and gold braiding, like a queen's robe, for her. They dress as though they are actors playing a scene—the quiet evening at home.

She slips into the closet to change. She always undresses in the closet.

"You know my mother used to do that," he says while she's gone.

Red. She has a dozen red housedresses, cocktail pajamas, leisure suits. The Hummingbird, the elf, the red pepper, cherry tomato, royal highness, power and blood.

"Why is the soup always cold?"

"So you won't burn yourself," she says.

He coughs during dinner, half-choking.

"Chew before you swallow," she says.

After dinner she pops one of his movies into the VCR. A walk down memory lane is supposed to be good for him, it is supposed to be comforting to see things from his past.

"Do you recall my premiere in Washington?"

"Your inaugural? January 20, 1981?"

"Now that was something." He stands up. "I'd like to thank each and every one of you for giving me this award."

"Tonight it's *Kings Row*," she says.

He gets a kick out of watching himself—the only hitch is that he thinks everything is real, it's all one long home movie.

"My father-in-law-to-be was a surgeon, scared the hell out of me when he cut off my legs."

"What are you talking about?" she asks, offended. "Dr. Loyal never wanted to hurt you," she said. "He liked you very much."

"Where's the rest of me?" he screams. "Where's the rest of me?" He's been so many different people, in so many different roles, and now he doesn't know where it stops or starts— he doesn't know who he is.

"What movie are we in?"

"We're not in a movie right now, this is real," she says, moving his dinner tray out of the way, reaching out to hold his hand.

"What time does the flight get in?"

"You're home," she says. "This is your home."

He looks around. "Oh yeah, when did we buy this place?"

At eight, Soledad comes in with her knitting, trailed by Philip with a plate of cookies, four glasses of milk.

Philip flips on the game and the four of them settle in on the king-sized bed, Philip, the President, she, and Soledad, lined up in a row, postmodern Bob & Carol & Ted & Alice. When the game begins, the President puts his hand over his heart and starts to sing.

"Oh say can you see . . ."

"Did you see that?" Soledad asks him. "He had that one on the rebound."

Philip, wanting to practice his reflexology, tries it on the President. He slips off the President's bedroom slippers and socks.

"Hey, quit tickling me." The President jerks his feet away. Philip offers his services to her.

"Oh, I don't know," she says. "My feet aren't in good shape. I haven't had a pedicure in weeks." She pauses. "What the hell," she says, kicking her slippers off. He is on the floor at the bottom of the bed. "That feels fantastic," she says after twenty minutes.

Soledad is crocheting a multicolored afghan to send to her mother for Christmas.

"What color next?" she asks the President. "Blue or orange?"

"Orange," the President says.

At night she is happy to have them there; it is a comfort not to be alone with him, and he seems to enjoy the company.

He sits on his side of the bed, picking invisible lint off himself.

"What are you going for there?" Philip asks.

"Bugs," he says. "I'm crawling with bugs."

Philip uses an imaginary spray and makes the spraying sound. Philip sprays the President and then he sprays himself. "You're all clean now," Philip says. "I sprayed you with disinfectant." The President stops picking.

At a certain point he gets up to go to the bathroom.

"He's getting worse," she says when he's gone.

They nod. The slow fade is becoming a fast forward.

He is gone a long time. After a while they all look at each other. "Are you all right?" she calls out.

"Just give me a minute," he says. He comes out of the bathroom with black shoe polish all over his face and red lipstick in a circle around his mouth. "My father used to do this one for me," he says, launching into an old Amos 'n' Andy routine.

"What did you use?" she asks, horrified.

"Kiwi," he says.

"I'm sorry," she says to Soledad, mortified that she is having to watch. Luckily, Soledad is from the islands and doesn't quite understand how horrible it is.

At eleven, Philip puts the rail on his side of the bed up, turns on the motion detector pad on the floor, tucks him in, and they call down to the gatehouse and tell them that the package is down for the night.

"Good night," she says.

"See you in the morning," Soledad says.

She stays up for a while, sitting next to him reading while he sleeps. This is her favorite part of the night. He sleeps and she can pretend that everything isn't as it is, she can pretend this is a dream, a nightmare, and in the morning it will all be fine.

She could remove herself, live in another part of the house and receive reports of his progress, but she remains in love with him, profoundly attached. She doesn't know how to be without him, and without her, he is nothing.

The motion detector goes off, turning on the light by her side of the bed. It is six-thirty in the morning.

"Is this conversation being taped?" He speaks directly into the roses, tapping his finger on the open flower as if testing the microphone. Petals fall to the floor. "Who's there? Is someone hiding over there?" He picks up the remote control and throws it into the billowing curtains.

"Hey, hey," she says, pushing up her eye mask, blinking. "No throwing."

"Go away, leave us alone," he says.

She takes his hand and holds it over the vent.

"It's the air," she says, "the air is moving the curtains."

He picks up the red toy telephone that he carries around everywhere—"just in case."

"I can't get a goddamned dial tone. How can I launch the missiles if I can't get a dial tone?"

"It's early," she says. "Come back to bed." She turns the television on to the morning cartoons, pulls her eye mask down, and crawls back into bed.

He is in the bathroom with the water running. "There's someone around here who looks familiar."

She pops her head in. "Are you talking to me?"

"Yes," he whispers. "That man, I can't remember that man's name." He points at the mirror.

"That's you," she says.

"Look, he waves and I'm waving back."

"You're the one waving."

"I just said that."

She notices an empty bottle of mouthwash on the sink. "Did you spill your mouthwash?"

"I drank it," he belches. Hot, minty-fresh air fills the bathroom.

In the morning, she has to locate him in time and space. To figure out when and where he is, she runs through a list of possible names.

"Honey, Sweetheart, Running Bear, Chief, Captain, Mr. President."

He stands before her, empty, nonreactive. She sticks a finger first into one ear and then the other, feeling for his hearing aid, they're both in, she plucks one out, cranks up the volume until it squeals.

"I'm checking the battery," she yells. "Can you hear me?"

"Of course I can. I'm not deaf." He takes the hearing aid from her and stuffs it back into his ear, putting it into the ear that already has one.

"Wrong ear," she says, fishing it out. She starts again. "Mr. President, Sir, Rough Rider, Rick, Daddy, Dutch." There is a flicker of recognition.

"Now that sounds familiar."

"Do you know who you are?"

"Give me a clue."

She continues. "Mr. P. Junior, Jelly Bean."

"Rings a bell."

"Jelly Bean?"

"That's me."

"Oh. Jelly Bean," she says, relieved to have found him. "What's new?" She hands him his clothing one piece at a time, in order, from under to outer.

Soledad rings a bell.

"Your breakfast is ready." She urges him down the hall. "Send the gardener in when he gets here," she instructs Soledad as she steps into a morning meeting with Philip and the agents.

"Don't call him Mr. President anymore—it's too confusing. It's best not to use any particular name; he's played so many roles, it's hard to know where he is at any given moment. This morning he's responding to Jelly Bean and talking about things from 1984."

"We're not always sure what to do," the head agent says, "how far to go. Yesterday he cleaned the pool for a couple of hours, he kept taking the leaves out, and whenever he looked away we just kept dumping them back, the same leaves over and over."

She nods.

"And then there were the holly berries. He was chewing on the bushes," the agent says.

"Halle Berry? George and Barbara?" Philip asks.

"The shrubbery—like a giraffe he was going around eating—" The agent stops in mid-sentence.

Jorge, the gardener, is standing in the doorway. He has taken off his shoes and holds them in his hand. He curtsies when he enters.

"Thank you," she says. She takes out a map and lays it on the table for everyone to see. "We need a safer garden; this is a list of the plants—they're all nontoxic, edible."

In the distance there is a heavy thump. The phone rings. She pushes the speakerphone button.

"Yes?"

"The President has banged into the sliding glass door."

"Is he hurt?

"He's all right—but he's got a bump on his head."

She sends Philip to check on him and she, Jorge, and the agents go into the yard and pace off where the wandering garden will be.

"Everything poisonous has to come out," she says. "Azaleas, birds of paradise, calla lilies, and daffodils. No more holly berries, hydrangea, tulips, poppies. No wisteria. No star-of-Bethlehem."

Jorge gets down on his knees, ready to begin.

She stops him. "Before you get dirty. I need you to put a lock on my dressing room door."

He is in the sunroom with a bag of ice on his face.

"Are you in pain?" she asks. He doesn't answer. "Did you have a nice breakfast?"

Again he belches, mint mouthwash.

"It won't happen again," Philip says, using masking tape to make a grid pattern on the sliding glass door, like a hurricane warning, like an Amish stencil in a cornfield, like the bars of a cattle crossing. "For some reason it works—they see it as a barrier and they don't cross it."

"Soledad, may I have a word?" She refrains from saying more until they are out of the room. "We need to make a few changes."

"I will miss you very much," Soledad says.

"It's time to get the house ready," she says, ignoring the comment, taking Soledad from room to room, pointing out what's not needed, what has to go in order to make life simpler, less confusing, safer.

"Put it away, send it to storage, keep that for yourself, this goes and this goes and this goes. Up with the rug, out with the chair."

They put safety plugs in every outlet, toddler latches on every cabinet. She moves quickly, as though time is limited, as though preparing for a disaster, a storm front of some sort.

"Send someone to one of the thrift shops and get a couple of Naugahyde sofas and some chairs."

"But you have such nice furniture," Soledad says.

"Exactly."

"Are we expecting a hurricane?" he asks, passing through. "I saw the boy taping up the window."

He knows and he doesn't know.

Jorge is in the bedroom, putting a huge combination lock on the dressing room door.

"Do we have any white paint?" She asks Jorge.

"No, Señora."

"We'll need some," she says. "Until then use this." She hands Soledad a bottle of Maalox. "Paint his mirror with it. Use a sponge if there isn't a brush. Put it on thick, so he can't see himself. It may take a couple of coats."

He is alone with Philip. They are in the kitchen, making chocolate chip cookies—slice and bake. The President plays with a hunk of dough, molding it into a dog.

"There are a couple of things I wanted to ask you, if you don't mind."

The President nods. "Go ahead, Tom."

"Who were your heroes?"

"Tarzan and Babe Ruth."

"Who was the most exciting person you ever met?"

"That would have to be Knute Rockne. I used to play ball with him. One hell of a guy."

"And in that whole Iran Contra thing, what was the bit about using the chocolate cake as a bribe?"

"Funny you mention it." He tilts his head, adopting the interview pose of careful consideration. "I was just thinking about her last night." He pauses. "You know, Bob, America is a country of families, companies, individuals who care about each other. This is another of those unavoidable tragedies, but in the end . . . It's them I worry about, the people who are out there."

"Any regrets?"

"I never walked on the moon. I was a little too old, they gave the part to another fella." He eats a clump of dough. "Listen," he says. "When I come to, everything will be fine, we'll get back on course. We're strong people, Mike, we'll get through."

She is online, catching up. The king of Toda has died and all the first ladies are going to the funeral. She can't leave him alone. "Now's not the time," she e-mails her secretary. "Tell them I have the flu, so no one gets suspicious."

She checks into the Alzheimer chat rooms.

—Her life must be a living hell. Imagine having everything in the world, all that help, and still you're on a sinking ship.

—She's an inspiration, how gracefully they handled it, and that letter he wrote about going off into the sunset.

—Do you think she even sees him? Does he recognize her? What condition is he in? We never hear a word.

They are talking about her. She is tempted to chime in, to defend herself. She wants to say, I am N.R. and you know nothing about my life.

—Think of all the people she got to meet and all the free clothes. She got a good deal. It's more than enough for one life-time."

—Got to go, Earl just wet himself. It's one thing when it's a twenty-two-pound infant the size of a turkey, it's another when it's a two-hundred-forty-pound man the size of a sofa.

She pedals faster. She's gone about thirty miles, when EZRIDER sends her an instant message.

—Where did you disappear to, EZ wants to know? Hope I didn't scare you.

—Telephone rang. Long distance.

—Where did we leave off?

—You were taking me for a ride on a Ferris wheel, we were high above it all . . .

There is a knock at her door. She ignores it. It comes again, harder.

"What the hell is it?"

The door opens. It's one of the agents. "Sorry to interrupt, but the President has disappeared."

She continues pedaling.

"We can't find him. We've searched the house, the perimeter, and Mike and Jeff are going up and down the block on foot." Mike and Jeff, he says—it sounds like Mutt and Jeff. "Should we call the police?"

She logs off, calmly gets off the bike, and punches the panic button on the wall. They all come running.

"Who last saw him, where, and when?"

"We were baking cookies about twenty minutes ago, the last batch just went into the oven, he said he had to go to the bathroom," Philip says.

"He was in the yard," one of the agents says, "relieving himself against a tree. That was maybe twenty-five minutes ago."

"He's eloped," Philip says. "It happens all the time, they have the urge to go, and then, as if summoned, they're gone."

"How many cars do we have?" she asks.

"The sedan, the van, Soledad's, and mine," Philip says.

"Divide into teams. Philip, you go on foot, I'll go with Soledad, does everyone have a cell phone?"

They quickly get their phones and exchange numbers.

"Those lines aren't secure," the agent says.

"No hysterical calls," she says. "Code name Francine."

She hurries out to the driveway and into Soledad's old red Mercury.

"We can't send you without an agent."

"Your agents can't find my husband," she says, slamming the door, missing the man's fingers by an eighth of an inch.

"We should call the police."

"The last thing we need to do is draw attention to what Keystone cops you are," she says, signaling to Soledad to start the engine.

"I think we're required to by law," one of the younger agents says. "We've never had a President disappear."

"Oh sure we have," one of the older men says. "We just don't talk about it. John Kennedy was gone for seventy-two hours once and we didn't have a clue."

She and Soledad take off. They see Mike down the street, talking to the Bristol Farms deliveryman, and Jeff following the mailman from house to house.

"Take a right," she says, and she and Soledad go up the hill, looking for signs.

Philip moves from door to door with an old glossy head shot. He rings the bell and holds the head shot in front of the electric eye. "Have you seen this man?" he asks, and then repeats the question in Spanish.

It can't end here, with him disappearing, the Amelia Earhart of politics. She is in the car with Soledad, imagining stories of mysterious sightings, dinner parties with him as the prize guest, him being held hostage in a Barcalounger in some faux paneled recreation room. She imagines him being found months later, when they get tired of taking care of him and pitch him out of a car in the Cedars-Sinai parking lot in the middle of the night, dirty and dehydrated.

They come upon a dog walker with eight dogs on eight different leashes, each dog a statement of sorts.

"Have you seen anyone walking around here? We've misplaced an older white man."

The dog walker shakes her head. "No one walks—if they want to walk, they get on the treadmill and watch TV."

They climb up St. Cloud, higher still. She remembers when she first came to Hollywood in the late 1940s as a young actress. She remembers going to parties at these houses, before they were married, when they used to spend evenings with Bill and Ardis Holden, when Jimmy Stewart lived on Roxbury Drive. She recalls the first time she visited Frank Sinatra's place on Foothill Road. She is reading it all now, like a map of the stars' homes.

The air is unmoving, smog presses down, hanging like a layer of dust waiting to fall, sealing them in. Soledad's car doesn't have air-conditioning; they drive with the windows down, it's the first time she's been in real air in years. She is sweating, there's a clammy glow to her skin.

Mike and Jeff wind downhill toward Westwood, UCLA, and Beverly Hills.

"Have you seen Ronald Reagan?"

"You might want to check on the quad—a lot of people were going over there, there's a puppet show or something."

"Ollie-ollie-oxen-free," Philip yells down the street. "Come out, come out, wherever you are. Come on down, The Price Is Right."

The Bel Air police pull him over. "Where do you belong?"

"At 668. I'm the President's personal trainer."

"You're the trainer?"

Philip pulls out his card. "Yes, the trainer. Now if you'll excuse me." He walks on, singing loudly, "hi-de-hi, hi-de-ho."

She is panicked that someone has him, she worries that they won't know who he is, they won't treat him well. She worries that they know exactly who he is and they won't give him back. She worries that he is wondering who he is.

"We had a dog who disappeared," she tells Soledad. "There was something about it that was horrible, the idea that he was out there somewhere, suffering, hurt, lost, wanting to get home and unable to."

"He can't have gotten far," Soledad says.

She has never told anyone, not even herself, but there are times lately when she just wishes it was over. As there is less and less of him, it becomes more painful, and she wishes it would end before he is no longer a man, but a thing, like a potted plant. She imagines making it happen, hastening the process, putting him out of her misery—she can't go on like this forever.

The cell phone rings. It's a conference call from the agents.

"Mike and Jeff are at the circle by the Beverly Hills Hotel. They believe they see Francine. She's out there in the middle of the circle directing traffic and apparently doing a pretty good job of it. They're waving at him—I mean her—and she's waving back. They're parking now and walking over. Yes, we have Francine. Francine has been found."

She is back at the house when the white van pulls through the gate.

He gets out, wearing an orange reflective safety vest.

"Where'd he get that?"

"We don't know."

She puts her hand in his pockets; there's money—singles and a five.

"Did someone take you away? Did someone give you a ride?"

"I got tips," he says.

The Bel Air police pull up with Philip in the back of the car. "Sorry to bother you," one of the cops says.

The agents grab the President, like a mannequin, and protectively pull him behind the van for cover.

"Do you know this man?" the cop asks.

"Has he done something wrong?" she asks.

"He was out, walking and singing, and he has a glossy photo of your husband and, well, we thought he looked a little like John Hinckley."

"He's our trainer," she says.

"That's what he said. And you're sure about that?"

"Quite."

"All right then, I'm sorry." The cop gets out, lets Philip out of the back of the car, and unlocks the handcuffs. "You can never be too careful."

"Of course you can't. Thank you."

"How did he get all the way to Beverly Hills?" Philip asks, when he finds out where they found him.

"I don't think he walked," she says.

She is livid. She wants to take him and shake him and tell him that if he ever does that again she's sending him away, putting him in a home under lock and key.

Instead she goes inside, picks up the phone, and calls Washington. "Head of the Secret Service, please, this is Nancy Reagan on the line."

"Can I have him return?" his secretary says.

"No."

"One moment, please."

The head of the service comes on the line. She reads him the riot act, starting calmly and working her way up. "I don't know what kind of agency you're running . . ." By the time she's finished she is screaming and the man on the other end is blithering. "How many men have you got there? We'll do a full investigation. I'll replace the whole crew. I don't know what to say. Maybe they weren't thinking. Maybe they're burned out."

"Burned out . . . You're supposed to be the best in the world and the man wandered away from his own home." She slams the phone down.

Philip helps him take a shower and change into clean clothing—jeans and a cowboy shirt. Philip has a cowboy hat for him, a toy guitar, and a piece of rope. They are in the backyard doing rope tricks.

"I've upset Mother," he says.

"It's all right, Chief, you gave us all quite a scare."

She is brittle, flash-frozen. And she has a backache. She takes a couple of aspirin and tries to catch her breath.

Later, he is in the bedroom, sitting on the floor playing with his toy guitar.

She goes to the padlock, starts spinning the numbers, one to the right, two to the left. She takes a sharp breath, makes an odd sound, turns around, gives him a surprised look—and falls face down on the floor. The sound is like a plank of light wood; there's a distinct snap—her nose breaking, her beak bending to the side.

"The hummingbird is down, the hummingbird is down." The call goes out when Philip finds her.

He rolls her over and attempts CPR. "Someone dial 911— dial 911," he shouts.

"That man is kissing Mother," he says, strumming his guitar.

Philip's breath, his compressions are useless. The paramedics arrive and try to jump-start her. Her body bounces off the floor, ribs snap. They are about to call for backup when Soledad steps forward, living will in hand, and tells them to stop. "No heroic measures," she says. "It's enough."

Soledad calls Dr. Sibley, who arranges for someone to meet them at Saint Johns, and they slide her into a garment bag, and discreetly tuck her into the back of Jorge's gardening truck under a pile of grass clippings. The ambulance stays out front while she is taken out the back. Jorge's Ever Green Gardening Service pulls away just as the news trucks pull up, raising their satellite dishes into the sky.

And he still sits on the bedroom floor strumming the guitar and singing an old cowboy song—"Yippee-ti-yi-yay, get along little dogies, you know that Wyoming will be your new home."

Also by A. M. Homes and available from Granta Books
www.grantabooks.com

MAY WE BE FORGIVEN

Harry has always envied his younger brother George – a
high-flying TV executive with two kids, a beautiful home
and a covetable wife – but Harry also knows that George is a
dangerous man with a murderous temper. When an adulterous
kiss at Thanksgiving prompts a chain of unexpected events,
George finally loses control, and the result is an act so shocking
that the brothers are hurled into entirely new lives,
ones in which they must both seek absolution.

'The narrative intensity of Jonathan Franzen's *The Corrections*
and the emotional punch of Siri Hustvedt's *What I Loved* ...
It's the best thing I've read this year' *Observer*

'This is the great American novel for our time' Jeanette
Winterson, *Guardian* Books of the Year

'Wonderful, wild, heartbreaking, hilarious and astonishing ...
A piercing, perceptive and deeply funny novel about the
nature of life, family and love' *Independent on Sunday*

'Homes's sharp, detailed prose teems with gloriously free, un-
airbrushed life' *Telegraph*

'Horribly funny and unexpectedly uplifting ... Sensational'
Daily Mail

'So engrossing that it makes you wish the real world would
go away and leave you to read ... A huge-hearted expansive
book, simultaneously nightmare-black and extremely funny'
Independent

Also by A. M. Homes and available from Granta Books
www.grantabooks.com

THIS BOOK WILL SAVE YOUR LIFE

Trading stocks and shares out of his beautiful LA home,
Richard Novak sees no one except his trainer, housekeeper and
nutritionist, who delivers regular supplies of macrobiotic low-carb
food. He is so out of touch with his feelings that his life has
slowed almost to a standstill. Following an attack of inexplicable
and excruciating pain that lands him in the emergency room,
Richard befriends Anhil the doughnut shop owner. His
solitary routine broken and his diet sabotaged by sugary
baked goods, Richard's dramatic emotional thaw begins.

'I think this brave story of a lost man's reconnection with the
world could become a generational touchstone, like *Catch-22*
or *The Catcher in the Rye* ... And hey, maybe it will
save somebody's life' Stephen King

'A delight' Ali Smith, *Daily Telegraph*

'Tender and unflinching' *New Statesman*

'Funny, peculiar, heartening, this book might not change your life,
but it could radically enhance a few days of it' *Financial Times*

'Weird and warm and wise and really rather wonderful'
Mark Haddon

Also by A. M. Homes and available from Granta Books
www.grantabooks.com

THE MISTRESS'S DAUGHTER

On the day that she was born in 1961, A. M. Homes was given
up for adoption. Her birth parents were a twenty-two-year-old
woman and an older, married man. Thirty-one years later, out
of the blue, they tracked her down. *The Mistress's Daughter* is
a riveting account of what happened next.

'A compelling, devastating and furiously good book written
with an honesty few of us would risk' Zadie Smith

'Gripping, salty, unnervingly good . . . a searing story packed
with questions of identity' *Daily Telegraph*

'A fascinating, immensely moving story from
a truly outstanding writer' *Elle*

'Utterly compelling . . . resonates for all of us who wonder how
much of us is inherited, how much learned' *Evening Standard*

'Never less than gripping . . . this book is a fine thing' *Guardian*

'Hilarious, brutally heartfelt and uncompromising' *Independent*

'A. M. Homes's new memoir is a gripping tale of identity and
family ties . . . beautifully structured and tautly written'
Harpers Bazaar

'An electrifying memoir . . . Ruthlessly exact and unadorned, it
is an endlessly generous, intelligent and compassionate account
of one person's biological rage for the truth' *Irish Times*